JONAS
AND THE
MOUNTAIN

A Metaphysical Love Story

Joanne
I hope you
enjoy your journey
with Jonas...
Namaste,
Janis

Also by
Janis Harper

(anthologies)
Body Breakdowns: Tales of Illness and Recovery
Emails From India: Women Write Home

JONAS
AND THE
MOUNTAIN

A Metaphysical Love Story

JANIS HARPER

SACRED STORIES
PUBLISHING

Books may be purchased through booksellers or by contacting Sacred Stories Publishing.

Author photo by Michael Crawford.
Icons made by Pixel perfect from www.flaticon.com.

Jonas and the Mountain: A Metaphysical Love Story
Janis Harper

Tradepaper ISBN: 978-1-945026-80-5
Electronic ISBN: 978-1-945026-81-2

Library of Congress Control Number: 2021940986

Published by Sacred Stories Publishing, Fort Lauderdale, FL USA

For my mother Lily

We are always seeking ourselves.

— Anamika

CONTENTS

I: THE MOUNTAIN

(Earth)

A damsel with a dulcimer
In a vision once I saw:
It was an Abyssinian maid
And on her dulcimer she played,
Singing of Mount Abora

— Samuel Taylor Coleridge, from "Kubla Khan"

CHAPTER 1

Either the world exists, or it doesn't. Jonas drops into meditation easily, like a pebble into a deep pool falling down, down into the quiet dark. The light flickering of thoughts occasionally nudge at the edge of his consciousness, but mostly there is silence. Stillness. Nothing.

A deep breath expands his lungs, and he feels the welcome peace fill him, palpable, soft. And although he doesn't think this, because he isn't thinking, it feels like pure relief. Or maybe he is aware of the feeling when those flickers of thoughts filter down like wavering ribbons of light from the surface into the depth of his still pool. Relief. One flicker. The awareness of the slowing down of breath. Another flicker.

Either there is something out there, or it's all in here and reflected out there. The world mirroring our own inner landscape, allowing us to meet what we need to. The world as symbol, metaphor, always personally meaningful if you can see it, if you can understand, interpret the symbols.

This is what Jonas's post-graduate English degree in literary criticism was good for. He was adept at interpretation. He could apply the same skills he learned to analyze metaphor, symbol, plot, theme, and structure in literary fiction to his own life, another kind of fiction. What is the overarching theme? Main conflict? Important metaphors? Repeating symbols?

In life as in literature, repetition is very important, a big clue, pointing to issues that are uniquely yours. Repetition can indicate theme, and theme gives a life shape, separates it from others, creates individuality, or at least the illusion of it.

What's the theme of Jonas's life? The major theme? For a period of three years, the theme seemed to be betrayal. Betrayed by his wife of ten years, by the college he gave seven years of his life to as a sessional instructor, by his best friend. Everything fell apart, one after another in close succession, like a line of dominoes falling down. No, dominoes don't create a sturdy structure, and Jonas's life used to feel sturdy. Maybe it was more like an earthquake that shook a house down to shambles on the ground. Or a tornado that swept it up in its vortex, bits and pieces of staircase, table legs, and light fixtures flying around.

Nothing he did for a few years was right. His whole world looked wrong; he was wrong. Obviously, "the universe" was banging him on the head, trying to get his attention. No, wrong way! Stop! But it wasn't until he had nothing, not until his life was unrecognizable, that he finally stopped fighting for himself (or was he fighting *with* himself?) and heeded the call.

He never asked himself, "Why me?" People who did that seemed to not understand something fundamental, that being what you imagine to be "a good person" doesn't mean you aren't going to experience bad things. And why would you not want to experience it all? The whole life show, including the ugly parts? Why would you think you should be exempt from a whole realm of experience just because it doesn't feel good? Maybe there are some people who do feel like they're better than others. Maybe they are the ones who ask, "Why me? What did I do to deserve this?"

Or maybe there are those who naively believe that if they're being as good as they know how to be, nothing bad will happen. Cause and effect. Karma. Of course, Jonas didn't "deserve" it, any of it. He was the victim, any way you cut it. And there's another strange thing: why people believe that some people deserve what they get and others don't. You often hear this kind of thing said about murder victims: "She didn't deserve to die." What does that even mean? Anyhow. "Why not me?" is the better question.

Falling apart is common enough in literature. It's almost a requirement. And more often than not it precedes greater personal awareness, a never-before-imagined perspective, a setting out on a new path toward a new world. Jonas could see those possibilities after the fact, a long time after. At the time, he could barely see a thing; he just concentrated on getting through each day, which took all of his attention and effort. But that's how stories end: crisis is reached, conflict is resolved, denouement occurs, and the protagonist walks away changed, into a new, better life.

So, did he have to go through all that to get here? Where is here?

Sitting with thirty other people at the feet of his guru, D, in the open-air meditation hall in an ashram at the foot of a holy mountain in India. And obviously not meditating anymore. His dark still pool is now all lit up by these thoughts. Just let them go, Jonas. It's okay. Be here now. He breathes in "here," he breathes out "now."

Jonas drops again into the deep, dark pool. He feels his body relax, his shoulders fall, his stomach muscles unclench, his breath slow. Relief. Here comes the soft peace.

CHAPTER 2

Two months before Jonas found himself in India, something unusual occurred. Sunk deeply into a familiar stagnant pool of limiting thoughts, he came up for air and heard himself crying out, Where do I go from here? And an answer came.

Where are you now?

The voice seemed to come from somewhere, but he couldn't determine the location. Was it outside his body, over there to the left? Or inside of him somehow. In thin, ringing tones he both heard and saw the words, each one turning into a balloon, disappearing in a moment and filled with that sound.

The ringing echoed in his head. Where am I now? What a question. Then Jonas knew the answer:

I am here.

That felt right. Here. He was just here. It was enough. He wasn't anywhere ugly; he wasn't on the brink of desperation; he wasn't stuck between a rock and a hard place. He had thought he was there, but he wasn't. He was just here.

Jonas felt something loosen inside. It was as if he had tightened the strings on his guitar too much but didn't know it, and now they were loosened. They could make sounds. He could hear the voice again, less thin this time, fuller, sweeter, a chord. Maybe A. Or D.

I am here too.

Jonas knew that if he thought too much about what was happening that he would get in the way of it. He felt an opening, the size and shape of an almond, and it started to vibrate. He knew somehow that there was a kind of backlog occurring, something—words? sounds? images?—was piling up. Jonas heard a popping sound, and felt himself recede.

Great galleons cross faraway oceans
to bring untold treasure and delicacies
to those gathered around bonfires
outside the caves that are their homes.
Time is measured by the motions
of currents and wind and moon.
Moods allow for rhythms of feeling
that synchronize with the wonders of nature.

Why has this boat come in?
There is little on it.
Where are the provisions, the food?
This one is not bringing in but carrying away,
and there are some who may choose
to leave on this boat
and take it to a far-off shore
undreamed of in the measured moments
and pungent air in the caves.

CHAPTER 3

Anna was eleven years old when she started having nightmares—or "night terrors" as she overheard her mother whisper in her "concerned" voice to Auntie Joy on the telephone. They weren't just bad dreams with scary people in them chasing her. *Those* were bad dreams, or maybe even nightmares. "Night terrors" might just be the right term. They were terrifying, but not in a movie way, not like a horror movie-nightmare.

Anna was so afraid of having these "dreams" that before she went to sleep, she put out her colored felt pens and paper and asked her mom to tell her to draw a picture the next time they came. She knew she'd need help to get her out of her scary place and back to normal. Her mother had been bringing Anna to the living room to look out the window at the city lights of Vancouver as a way to get her out of it. But it didn't help. The darkness, the squares and pinpoints of light from the buildings across English Bay, out the huge window...all that kept her in her scary place. Even with her mom by her side, saying gentle things to her and putting her arm around her, Anna didn't come back to her "normal" self. She just heard her own voice coming from far away, through a long tunnel.

"God. Oh my God. Oh my God."

Anna tried to describe her night terrors one day to her mother, but could only say stupid-sounding stuff like, "It's like there's this one black hair, and it's at a normal distance away from me, then suddenly it's huge right in my face, then it's going back back back and it keeps going back, and the empty place where it was is huge in my face, but it's still back and there's no end."

Anna was not in time and space. She was not in her body. Dimensions appeared and disappeared. She glimpsed infinity. And when she did, of course it was too immense, too huge for her perceptive faculties. Waking up didn't take her out of it because it wasn't really a sleep-dream state. And she was overwhelmed because she didn't know what was happening to her—and that was the most frightening part.

In biological terms, Anna's pineal gland was opening. In Western science, which still finds the pineal gland mysterious, it supposedly regulates sleep-wake patterns and reproductive hormones. Rene Descartes called the pineal gland "the seat of the soul," and in many philosophies it is considered a portal to the spiritual world, a physiological "third eye." The opening of the pineal gland isn't uncommon in adolescence, and is often the precursor to creative pursuits, the flaring up of artistic passions. And in Anna's case, it was a creative time indeed: she was bridging worlds. She came tumbling through the portal. Her third eye opened wide and didn't blink. It was as if she were on top of a mountain and could see the entire lay of the land, everything, stretching out every which way she looked.

But it was also as if she were being given something that was almost too much for a person, for anyone with a body—much less a skinny little-girl body with long brown braids that curled at the ends and dark almond eyes that crunched up into crescent moons when she smiled. How can anyone experience such ineffable enormity, such expansiveness, such powerful creative energy; how can anyone see through transparencies in reality and into other dimensions just as real, and still be able to walk and talk and eat soda crackers with butter and play kick-the-can with the kids down the block?

It can be done. Anna did it. But as she grew through some very rocky teenage years into an adult, she was always aware that she was merely keeping up appearances. She'd inherited her mother's talent as an actress to mimic other people—more than mimic, to understand their motivation, why they said and did what they said and did. So she acted as if she were in the same play they were in. She was good: she could tell in an instant what part someone was playing and what part she should play in response. And she could play with the best of them—because she knew the range of motivations and emotions and which were appropriate for which scene and cast. She was good with language, too. (She had also inherited that from her mother, who had taught high school English after her acting career ended.) No one suspected a thing.

Anna the 25-year-old had several friends, a casual boyfriend, a job tending bar at a local watering hole, and the occasional role in a community theater production. She still had long brown hair, loose now and curly, and crunchy eyes. And she knew everything. She knew beyond a shadow of a doubt all of the answers to all of the big questions, all of the "whys" and even some of the "hows." She just didn't know what to do with all of it. So she hid it. She wanted to be liked, after all. She had inherited that from her mother too.

And it was so hard to express, for another thing. It was so different at its very roots from what others were saying. She had tried college for two years, and read eagerly, trying to find what she knew in literature, philosophy, science, psychology, religious studies. Anna was an excellent student and asked many good questions. She certainly *looked* like she was on an academic path. She then turned to the mystical and heretical, the metaphysical, the spiritual, the paranormal. Her friends saw the books on her coffee table. She certainly *looked* like she was on a spiritual, maybe even "new age-y," path. And she did find bits and pieces of what she knew to be true in various places: Eastern spirituality, Western mysticism, ancient Greek philosophy, neuroscience, quantum mechanics, metaphysics, channeling.

For Anna wasn't on any kind of path. She was retracing her steps, doing it backwards. As much as it looked that way to others, Anna was not looking for the truth. She already knew it, of course. She was looking for some discipline, some system, someone *else* to have come up with it, too. For how could she continue to live a life faking it all the time? She wanted to belong to a community—or, at least, she needed a way to be herself in the world. Being able to point to something else and say, yes, I'm that too, would be nice and normal. She'd have someone to really talk to. She began to envy religious people and political activists.

Sometimes she thought she would explode with all that she had to keep inside of her. So, occasionally, 25-year-old Anna would experiment, usually when she was having a drink or three after her shift at the bar was over: she consciously, albeit tipsily, fell out of character and told the truth when she was asked her opinion. And the results were usually disastrous. People got very angry. She occasionally tried this sober, too, in serious settings with open-minded, intelligent people. Same results.

So Anna took a different route. One day, she simply receded from the world. She all but disappeared from the face of it.

And this is how Anna, the little girl who sat in the dark with her mother on a living room couch, looking out at the city lights of Vancouver and uttering "Oh my God," became Anamika, the nameless one. And how she came to appear at the holy mountain of Arunachala in the state of Tamil Nadu, in the land of India.

CHAPTER 4

Jonas came out of what could be called a "trance," and shook himself. He grabbed the nearest pen and wrote down the words that he...heard? Felt? Saw? They seemed to form a kind of poem, though he's pretty sure no one in academia or in the literary community would call it one. He wasn't sure what to make of it, but there was something about it that he liked, some quality. What are *galleons*? He looked up the word. Wikipedia said, "A galleon was a large, multi-decked sailing ship used primarily by European states from the 16th to 18th centuries." That was it, the quality: it had an "old" feel, 18th century-ish maybe. Jonas himself would never use words like *delicacies* or *untold*. And the people in the caves? The boat is for *carrying away*, leaving for unknown shores, not for providing sustenance to the cave-dwellers, not toward maintaining a lifestyle. Interesting.

Measured moments. He liked that. *Time is measured by the motions / of currents and wind and moon.* There was some sense there. Perhaps time isn't a real thing or whatever in itself, but only a measurement we make. In the case of the poem that arrived, it is nature that dictates time, the movement of ocean currents and the moon and the way the wind blows. Or we use nature's movements as a measurement, a way of ordering our day-to-day lives. There is night and day, after all. And seasons. But maybe those are not passages of time until we make it so.

The more Jonas studied this "poem" that came out of him without him knowing, the more excited he got. It was a different kind of excitement than he felt when he discovered a new way of looking at a poem in a literary analysis course. His body was actually tingling. But his mind seemed calm. What just happened, anyway? Of course, having studied English literature at university, the first person he thought of was Coleridge and the much-discussed way he wrote his famous "Kubla Khan" poem, one of his best. In Coleridge's own words,

> The Author continued for about three hours in a profound sleep, at least of the external senses, during which time he has the most vivid confidence, that he could not have composed less than from two to three hundred lines; if that indeed can be called composition in which all the images rose up before him as things, with a parallel production of the correspondent expressions, without any sensation or consciousness of effort. On awakening he appeared to himself to have a distinct recollection of the whole, and taking his pen, ink, and paper, instantly and eagerly wrote down the lines that are here preserved.

In university, Jonas always attributed Coleridge's "Kubla Khan" to the painkiller he'd taken before a nap. But obviously he hadn't thought about it much. Drugs usually don't enhance creativity, but stifle it. He knows that now. He knows that well, after taking whatever pain-numbing kind of drug he could get his hands on after Carla left him, then adding amphetamines when he had to get back to a regular teaching schedule. And he wasn't even trying to be artistically creative. The drugs seemed to wear away his very neural fibers so that just preparing his academic writing class felt like slogging through waist-deep mud.

You don't get this from drugs. Jonas knew the lingo, too: "automatic writing," even "channeling." But he didn't want to think about that now. He felt good.

Excited. Alive. Curious. Could it happen again? And what should he do with this poem thing?

Why has this boat come in?
. . . .
and take it to a far-off shore
undreamed of in the measured moments
and pungent air in the caves

∼

Jonas didn't really know why he was going to India, except that a friend was going and invited him along. Since he was growing tired of his job at the print shop and was feeling that a daily change in his life was on the horizon, to match the inner changes he was experiencing, he said yes. Why not? He had enough money saved and India was cheap. Besides, he hadn't traveled since he and Carla took a trip to a resort in Puerto Vallarta, which was the beginning of the end of their marriage.

Jonas didn't know what to do with these inner changes. He had had several more "experiences" where something shifted inside of him, he backed off (it was indeed almost like taking a nap!), and the next thing he knew there were these images rising up and he felt corresponding words toppling out of the images, sometimes slowly, other times rushing up like a fountain. Now he always had a pen or keyboard handy to take dictation. That's what it felt like: taking dictation. Often his eyes were closed, and he didn't know what was going on until after, when he read the words written.

But he hadn't heard that voice again, that other voice that seemed to talk directly to him and asked him where he was. And he didn't want to address the "poem-giver," ask him or her (or it?) questions. He was scared of the response. He didn't want to be a channeler, didn't want to be thrown into a strange new world. What would happen next? People would want things from him, want to hear what the poem-giver said. He would be labeled a "psychic," a "medium," a "channeler." He knew about famous channelers who looked weird and spoke in strange voices when they were doing their thing. It polarized people, divided them into camps of skeptics and believers.

Jonas wanted a quiet life. He didn't want to have to defend himself. He had enough of his own problems, thank you very much. He liked these apocryphal poems, though. They interested him, and made him feel something. Different. Special. Like there was indeed more to life. But he didn't tell anyone about them. Except Bruce.

Jonas's travel companion was a fellow worker at Kinko's. Bruce never went to university but read voraciously, and often over a print job when it was just the two of them working overtime Jonas and Bruce would have long conversations about what Bruce was currently reading. Jonas admired and envied Bruce's *joie de vivre*. He was Jonas's age, mid-thirties, and had spent his life seemingly enjoying himself—working happily at various joe jobs while traveling intermittently to hot countries, surfing, climbing, and having casual relationships with hot women. He had an innocence and enthusiasm about life, and believed in everything. He was lucky, too. He hadn't experienced the dark side like Jonas had. Bruce was also Jonas's physical opposite—a perpetually tanned, blond, muscular, square-jawed, Greek-god type, a contrast to Jonas's serious academic-nerd look: tall, pale, and skinny, with a long face under a mop of unruly dark hair. People think he's Jewish, but he's not.

Lately, Bruce had been on a serious spiritual kick, learning to meditate and chant, and reading about Buddhism and, more recently, Hinduism. Jonas could contribute to the conversation because he had taken a couple of courses in Eastern Religious Studies at university, and did some yoga and even meditated sometimes. Bruce had read some of the *Bhagavadgita* and various books about eastern mysticism and philosophy, like *Autobiography of a Yogi* by Paramahansa Yogananda. After he read a book from the 1930s, *A Search in Secret India*, by Paul Brunton, he got especially interested in Advaita Vedanta philosophy, or non-dualism, and a prominent Indian sage who died in 1950 named Sri Ramana Maharshi who had lived in a cave on the side of a mountain for a couple of decades. As far as he knew, lots of people (and animals and insects!) were drawn to this quiet man who just liked to be alone and meditate in his cave. So when things got too busy and his group of followers got too large, he moved to another cave. Now there's a whole school of thought and teachings and a "lineage" of guru-disciples originating with Ramana, and he's considered to be one of India's greatest sages of all time. A real master.

Ramana's own guru was the mountain in whose caves he lived. Mt. Arunachala is supposedly a very special holy mountain in India. Jonas didn't understand a lot about this place. For instance, how can a mountain be a guru? And what's so special about this mountain that it draws all manner of spiritual seekers and gurus and sages from all over the world? And apparently it always has. The mountain is said to be the god Shiva incarnated. But in Jonas's knowledge of India, Shiva seemed to be incarnated everywhere. It's also called the "magnet mountain" because it draws people to it, and many find it difficult to leave. And it's supposed to be filled with iron ore.

Well, Jonas would soon find out for himself, because Mt. Arunachala is where he and Bruce were headed.

~

The cab ride to Tiruvannamalai from Chennai was four long, hard hours, and Jonas was still suffering from the two-day air travel from Vancouver through London and Delhi to Chennai, in Tamil Nadu, India's large southeastern state. And then, upon arriving, the shock of it all: the incessant heat, the swarms of people, the filth, the smelliness, the cacophony of honking horns. It's true what they say: India is an endless assault on the senses.

Tiruvannamalai, or "Tiru" for short, looked like all the other dusty, dirty towns they'd driven through on the way to get here: cows, dogs, oxen, motorbikes, cars, rickshaws—and people—all weaving around each other on narrow garbage-strewn streets lined with tiny store fronts and food stalls. The difference in Tiru is that, in addition to the hundreds of Indians—women in brightly colored saris and men in plain lunghis—there were many white people walking around, dressed in traditional Indian clothes and riding motorbikes and bicycles. And another difference was the number of old Indian men draped in bright orange cloth, with long grey beards and knotted dreadlocky hair. "Sadhus, holy men," their cab driver said.

After Jonas and Bruce found a room in a travelers hotel, Mountain View Towers (apparently there were cost-free rooms at Ramana's ashram, but they were too tired to look into staying there), Jonas left Bruce napping in their room, and hiked up the four flights of stairs to the rooftop, where there was an open-air restaurant with cushions for seats and low tables on the cement floor. Jonas plunked himself down cross-legged on a cushion, grateful to be out of the car and sitting in a different position.

And there was the view, as advertised. Mt. Arunachala sat there, a nondescript lumpy red-brown hill, with some scrub on it and patches of rock. But as Jonas gazed up at it, wondering at its ordinariness, the tail end of his spine began to hurt. No wonder, he thought, my tailbone is aching after hours in the bumpy cab. But the sensation was different than an ache: it felt like there was a heavy weight in it. Sometimes after yoga when he was sitting and trying to meditate, he felt like this, like all of his body's energy was settling into his base chakra. Jonas's lower spine seemed to extend past his body and down down down into the earth, like the roots of a tree. He felt he would never move again; he was rooted to this spot. And that was somehow perfectly fine. He didn't want to go anywhere. More than that, he had no desire for anything. His tiredness vanished—all he was aware of was the deep, heavy sensation at the root of his body. And a feeling of immensity. And peacefulness. Immense peace. He is here. After all.

~

Jonas and Bruce had been in Tiru a few days, and were getting used to being in the presence of this mountain. And Jonas didn't experience anything as strong as that first time he met Arunachala. Sometimes he felt moments of relief when he turned his gaze toward it, but most of the time he and Bruce were caught up in learning how to navigate daily life here.

In the restaurants popular with all the white spiritual seekers that flocked to this place, Jonas saw that there were notice boards covered in little posters advertising some guru or other, or sessions of yoga, reiki, massage, crystal healing, you name it. There were pictures on these posters of the gurus—or teachers, which is what gurus are—and most of them were of white foreigners, men and women, and on the posters were listed websites and testimonials, and short descriptions of how these gurus can "open your heart," "lift the veils," "bring you into bliss." They advertised free "satsang," which Jonas learned was like a little class where you can ask the guru questions and maybe do some meditation or something. And they advertised retreats that lasted days or weeks, and cost real money, not rupees. The notice boards were pretty much exactly like the ones he'd seen at metaphysical bookstores and health food stores in Vancouver.

He found all of this quite irritating and, well, flaky. And there were too many choices. It was overwhelming. Who were all these people who were so sure they had the answers and also so sure that they had to tell others? Tiru was like a Spiritual Disneyland or New Age Carnival: anything your soul needs is right here, step right up! Spiritual tourism, he thinks it's called. And he expected it in India, but not like this. Wasn't he supposed to go sit quietly at the feet of an enlightened old Indian man? Like Ramana?

And it seems that all of these professional spiritual seeker types have nothing else in their lives but this hunger for something more, and their lives are all about following the spiritual path, going on retreats, seeking enlightenment. Where do they get the money for it? Don't they work? Some of them seem to bop about from one teacher to another, and Jonas has heard them discuss with each other who's good, whose retreat they've "done," and sometimes which ashram they've come from and where they're going next. Jonas learned that there are a handful of non-dual teachers who are the popular ones, the rock star gurus.

All of this retreat hopping and guru-comparison shopping didn't seem to be very spiritual to Jonas. He could understand the hunger part. But who's to say this hunger wasn't for avoiding what they have, escaping their own personal pain? Running away from life? Spiritual meds. Bliss bandaids. He figured it's better than getting addicted to drugs. But wasn't this just another kind of addiction? Jonas had by now spoken with many of these seekers, most of whom were kind, gentle, and sincere—and some were even very intelligent and had left behind highly accomplished professional lives—and he was feeling confused. He wished he could go somewhere for a beer, but this town—being holy and all—had no alcohol in it. So he just gave in to his feeling of confusion. He didn't try to resolve it, or escape it. He couldn't if he tried.

Jonas decided all he could do was to surrender to India, to being here in this crazy place, because if he didn't, he'd probably be forced to anyway. This Satsang Central thing was certainly weird and unexpected. But more than that, so much of being in India was just really hard, like doing the daily little things that are so easy in Canada: trying to find an ATM, then trying to find an ATM that worked, trying not to get killed crossing a street, trying not to run into a cow, trying to find a restaurant that could make eggs over-easy as he liked them, trying not to crave hamburgers and bacon, trying to talk to all these strangers, trying to avoid the insistent beggars and the cow shit everywhere and always the blazing sun on his pale skin. Mostly he tried not to get frustrated by all of these things.

Then he discovered that the frustration arose out of the *trying* itself. So he decided to just stop trying. And be open to whatever India was offering in the moment.

And once he did that, he felt a relief akin to gazing up at Mt. Arunachala. He had made peace with being here. He could breathe again.

~

Although Jonas didn't know why he had spontaneously agreed to come here with Bruce, he did know that he definitely wasn't the "spiritual seeker" type. He just wasn't looking. Besides, he didn't think he believed in gurus. Or even enlightenment. Which is what a guru is good for, for getting you there. He couldn't get Van Morrison's song "Enlightenment" out of his mind. Van says he doesn't know what it is. Neither did Jonas.

But he did know that something was going on that he couldn't—and didn't want to—explain or even understand. These poems that "arrived" from somewhere (someone?) else. The way he dropped out of himself right before. And the strange language, tone, and content of these pieces. He'd considered seeing if he could publish any, or even gather them into a collection, a book, but it didn't seem right. They weren't really *his*; he wasn't the author. Yet, if Coleridge could do it…

And, heck, maybe all poetry—all art, for that matter—comes from elsewhere. You certainly don't use your mind when you create artistically; everyone knows that. "Inspiration": a drawing *in* from somewhere else, like drawing in breath. And breath is life. You die when you expire, breathe out. You become when you aspire, breathe in and out.

Breathing. Jonas was developing a new relationship to his breath, his breathing. In and out. What a magical process. Jonas hadn't been aware of it before. He, Jonas, wasn't breathing; he wasn't doing it. His breath moved through him *on its own*. It breathed him. He couldn't stop it or change it. He couldn't control his breath, not for any length of time.

He wasn't in control of something so intimate as his breath. Strange. Why hadn't he known this before? He wasn't in control of the very thing that allowed him to live. And if you're not in control of your life, then what do you control?

And it didn't matter what he did, it just continued to happen. The breathing went on. He never practiced it, either. He couldn't force it. Without being aware of it, for his entire life, he had trusted in something that he couldn't put a finger on, and trusted so entirely that he hadn't given it much thought. In fact, as soon as he started thinking about his breath, it stopped flowing easily. It became *labored*.

He had trusted in his breath. He had to. He trusted his breath now. His breath had been carrying him all along. Was still carrying him.

Jonas's breath carried him right to D. Or maybe it was the other way around.

Jonas's friend Bruce had become enamored of a little elderly Indian woman guru who was called Amma. There wasn't a poster about her satsang on the notice board, but word got out easily among the seekers. She was enlightened. And every morning he went to sit in a room with a hundred or so foreigners and meditate until this woman in a watermelon-colored sari slowly walked through the room, smiling slightly, and occasionally glancing at the people sitting cross-legged on the floor. Bruce said that when she looked at him—and apparently she always did, every time—he was filled with what he called indescribable bliss. (Maybe she looked at everyone, Jonas wondered privately. Was that even possible?)

Then Bruce, still feeling somewhat blissed out, spent the rest of the day at Ramana's ashram, and read at the library, sat in the meditation hall, or just wandered the quiet grounds barefoot among the peacocks, retracing Ramana's steps. Sometimes he trekked up the mountain and hung out in Ramana's caves. He told Jonas that he was thinking of moving out of Mountain View Towers and getting a free room at the ashram, eating with the devotees in the dining hall there, and maybe volunteering at the ashram bookstore. It appeared that Bruce, as usual, had gotten what he wanted. Jonas was happy for him, if a tiny bit envious. But he was not sure how happy he was that Bruce was moving on without him.

Jonas had attended a few satsangs and had had some cool experiences, especially with one Indian-Swiss guru called Mataji. When he meditated briefly in her presence (she taught that only five-minute meditations were best), he felt his head get so heavy it wouldn't stay upright but flopped over onto his chest. Once he even tried to hold his head up with his hands. During one of these brief meditations, he opened his eyes and looked at her, and her eyes immediately flashed open right into his from across the room. They held each other's gaze for at least a minute before she mumbled something and closed her eyes again. Jonas experienced an electric surge up his spine. She was pretty, too. Almost too pretty for a guru. It could be distracting.

On the way back to the hotel after satsang with Mataji, Jonas stopped to watch two Indian boys play a game with stones on the ground. It reminded him of crokinole, a game he used to play with his dad when he was little. It was one of the few activities Jonas remembered enjoying with his father, a high-powered businessman who never seemed to have enough time for him. The boys asked if he wanted to join them, but he said he had somewhere he had to be. As he walked away, he wondered if he said that as an excuse because, truthfully, he had no plans. Why wouldn't he want to play with them? And why would he lie?

At some point, he realized he had lost his way back to the hotel. The narrow streets twisted and turned, maze-like, and he had no idea which direction he was going in. He stopped in front of another hotel, a fancy looking one that boasted air conditioning. There was a little poster out front announcing a satsang that started in 15 minutes with a guru called "D." That's it. The letter D. Jonas wondered if the rest of the name had gotten accidentally erased.

Curious, and anticipating the chilled breeze of air conditioning, Jonas took the elevator to the room on the top floor, and entered. The room was indeed cool, much to Jonas's relief, and filled with the usual seekers, cross-legged and eyes closed, only here there were some older men and women sitting on chairs, too. And, sitting on a chair separate from the gathered group, Jonas could see the back of a man in the corner, facing a large window through which Arunachala loomed. Jonas found a cushion and sat. And breathed.

When D turned around, Jonas beheld a stocky Caucasian man around fifty-something, with a full beard and a good head of graying dark hair—shaggy but handsome in a professorial kind of way. Expecting to hear a lecturer's tones, he was taken aback by the quiet softness of D's voice when he spoke, as well as by his American accent. "Welcome."

During the next hour and a half, Jonas fell in love. And in recognition. Every word that came out of D's mouth seemed directed to him personally, and he understood everything D said deeply, as if he already knew it well. When D answered questions from the group, it was another kind of perfection. Jonas hadn't heard anyone as articulate as D, not even Jonas's best English profs. He reveled in how D used language, how he conveyed such seemingly complex, abstract notions with such searing simplicity. D's words went right in and touched him at his core. But most of all, Jonas was hit with what could only be called love. This bearded American dude seemed to radiate love and compassion for everybody. It was visceral. Some people cried in his presence. Everybody laughed.

Jonas couldn't take the smile off of his face. He didn't want this satsang to end.

CHAPTER 5

The time was always 11:11 in Anamika's world. Or so it seemed. Her mother had died at 11:11, and every single time Anamika glanced at the digital clock on the wall shelf of the small apartment she lived in, it was 11:11 AM or PM. Each time she smiled and said, "Hi Mom!" She felt her presence especially then, as surely as she felt the presence of the creatures that started to hang out on her doorstep.

Anamika looked Indian in India. Her eyes opened more, became rounder and wider, like Indian eyes. They lost their "crunch." And her olive skin was deeply tanned to a rich brown; her hair, still long and curly and dark, was naturally like Indian hair. Only now that she applied coconut oil to it, it smelled like Indian hair, too.

Anamika was given her name by an old orange-robed sadhu who found her sleeping by the side of the road nearby one of the many temples around Arunachala. They had hung out together, smoking beedies and meditating for several days. They didn't speak the same language. She never knew his name, and he didn't know hers (which she was on the brink of forgetting anyway). But when they parted one day, he put his hands together in respectful Namaste, and said, "Anamika." Later, she discovered its Sanskrit meaning: "the nameless one."

First it was a dog lying on her doorstep. Then another dog, and another one. Dogs roamed the streets here, bedraggled and homeless, so she figured they had found a comfy place to sleep on her stoop. Then some of the strange-looking Indian crows started hanging out there, too. Once a cow just stood in the street outside her place for a couple of hours. She seemed to be collecting a menagerie of local creatures outside her door. Anamika didn't mind. She'd been alone for she didn't know how long, and although she liked it that way, she also liked dogs.

After her bartender savings had run out, and she spent some time sleeping on the streets and in the temples and ashrams close to Arunachala, she found this little apartment beneath a travel agency, on the outskirts of Tiru, close to the mountain. It was cheap, she could keep a hot plate in it and cook her own food, and she made enough money to pay for it and daily necessities by helping out at the travel agency two days a week. Mostly she did errands, but sometimes she helped Ramu communicate with the travelers. He was originally from Nepal and spoke English well; it was more that she had to explain how things were done here. She communicated culture more than language. Perhaps Ramu's clients mistook her for an Indian woman. His business was booming, and travelers started coming from town to Ramu's Travel to book their trains, planes, and buses.

But she rarely socialized with the other foreigners. She wasn't in India to meet people. She was here so she could stop hiding herself from others who didn't know what she knew and definitely didn't want to know. She came, finally, to be herself. And she felt free for the first time. Authentic. Mt. Arunachala drew an odd assortment of people, and they were all looking for freedom of one kind or another. The odd time she spoke to someone in a shop or at a restaurant, she felt she could say anything and it would be accepted. She was just another oddity in the assortment.

And then there was the mountain. She loved it and didn't know why. It spoke to her in the day and sang her to sleep at night. She felt welcomed here. She was happy.

Anamika got used to the creatures on her doorstep, but when she opened her door one morning and found a couple around her age sitting there, dressed in baggy pants and long white kurtas, she was surprised. They were patting the dogs, and when she came out, they stood up and put their palms together in Namaste. Then they just sat back down and smiled, as if they were waiting for something. Anamika smiled politely and quickly walked past them, got on her scooter, and drove into town. When she returned an hour later with some groceries, they were still there.

They explained in German-accented English that they had heard about the woman who drew the creatures to her, and they were hoping she would talk to them. They wanted to listen.

"Talk to you? About what?" As Anamika asked the question, she already knew the answer.

"What you know," came the reply.

Anamika invited the German couple inside. When she deposited her groceries on the table in her little kitchen area, her eyes were drawn to the clock on the shelf. It was 11:11. Oh, Hi Mom!

Her mother died just before Anna herself disappeared into Anamika. Lily had been sick for quite a while, and she also had early-onset dementia, so she kept on forgetting she was sick and was always shocked to find herself in the hospital. After she returned to her comfortable assisted-living home, she promptly forgot she was ever hospitalized. She hated the idea of being sick, and she was terrified of dying. This hospital-home-forgetting scenario repeated over several months.

This last time was different. Her mother had had a stroke. One half of her face sagged, and she couldn't move one arm. She spoke clumsily and slowly out of one side of her mouth. She couldn't put on her usual happy face and act as if everything was great. Her actress persona had fallen off. She was very vulnerable.

Childlike. This touched Anna so deeply it hurt. She had never seen her mother so exposed. Anna felt a sharp tug on her heart when her mother looked at her from her hospital bed, eyes large and questioning, and shyly, tentatively, asked, "Do I live here now?" Lily didn't know what was going on. But Anna knew.

And Anna knew that she wasn't supposed to tell. She was supposed to play the game, act her part. So she cheerfully responded, "No, of course not. We're taking you home soon, back to your own lovely place!" That was indeed what the doctors thought would happen, too. Lily was recovering well from the stroke and would be home soon. Only Anna knew differently.

She knew it when they arrived in the ER two days before, when her mother was once again in A-fib right before she had the stroke, and amid the panic and distress Lily paused and exclaimed, "Anna! I think my mom's here. I mean *really* here. I can feel her. Is that possible? How can that be?" Then she slumped over.

She knew it when out the window of her mother's hospital room she saw a little rainbow connecting the sea in English Bay to the mountains behind downtown Vancouver. It was a short, low arc—not sweeping across the sky, but like a bridge. A colorful bridge of light situated among the other more solid bridges downtown. Anna pointed it out to her mother, who had always loved the mountains and the sea, had always insisted on living where she had "a view." The hospital room had a beautiful view.

Most of all she knew it when she sat quietly beside her mother, opened her inner senses wide, and listened with every part of her.

"Don't be scared. It'll be okay," Anna said. Anna wanted to help her mother make the transition, help her adjust her focal point from this life to another dimension. In other words, die. Anna knew these were the words her mother needed to hear. She also knew they could be taken on two levels. On one level, her mother would be comforted, thinking that she was going to recover, go home, and all would be as before. On another level... Anna hoped she would be comforted there, too. For Anna knew it really would be okay; she knew there was nothing to fear. And she knew that her mother knew she knew. Lily looked into Anna's eyes. Just looked.

"It'll be okay," Anna said.

Anamika turned her attention away from the clock on the shelf and toward the couple who had found a place on her floor to sit.

She looked at them for a while. And listened. When Anamika finally spoke, this is what she said: "This is what happens after death."

CHAPTER 6

Jonas slept long and deeply after he found D. When he finally opened his eyes the next morning, it was 11:11. Bruce had already gotten up and gone out. Jonas was alone. He felt good, anticipating seeing D again in his last "public" satsang. In a few days, there was a two-week retreat in an ashram a bit out of town, closer to the mountain. Jonas didn't know if he was going to go, if he could even afford it. He thought he'd wait until today's satsang and see how he felt. Or see what happened. Things just seemed to happen here.

As he swung his legs over the hard mattress and stood up, Jonas felt a pain in the center of his chest. He crumpled to the floor. Images of Carla filled him, and he felt that his breath was being drawn out of him, as if something was pulling it out from his belly, through his lungs, and out of his mouth. Attached to the breath came a sound, a wail. Jonas was sobbing with his whole body. Right there on the hard, tiled floor of his hotel room. He couldn't stop. He was never going to stop. It wasn't him doing it, it was his body. He had no control. Carla. How could you? How could you do this to *me*?

After what seemed like hours, the crying wound down by itself. His breathing slowly changed, and he felt a big space inside his chest. Did his heart just break wide open? He felt hollow and light. Jonas pushed himself off the floor and sat on the bed.

He'd never cried like this before. The closest he'd come was when his and Carla's dog Maxwell died. Then he melted into tears. And still does sometimes. That is grief, mourning. It has its own logic—hits you when you least expect it. And when his mother died he was not even three years old, too young to grieve her loss. He remembers a vague feeling of bewilderment. After he and Carla split—well, after she left him for Seb—he would cry sometimes, but mostly out of anger and frustration. And often because he felt sorry for himself.

This, this was different. He'd never cried like this over Carla. Maybe he was finally mourning the loss of their relationship, grieving for the death of their love. He hadn't done that yet; there was too much anger. Or maybe it had nothing to do with her. This felt like a purging. Was he finally mourning the death of his mother, too? All of the stuff that he hadn't done anything with, that was still inside of him, came out. It felt so…physical. The emotions were physical, moving on their own through his body. Emotion. Motion. Movement.

Feeling light and loose, and with an open feeling in his chest (is this what "open-hearted" really means, he wondered; is it all just about the body?), Jonas got dressed and found his way to D's last public satsang. He had just enough time to pick up a chai and samosa from a street stall along the way.

CHAPTER 7

"I don't speak out of a particular tradition. I'm not going to sound like these wonderful Indian masters, though you'll recognize some commonalities. They speak truth, too. But I'm not going to talk of enlightenment or union with the divine. I won't tell you how to transcend the world of duality, transcend suffering. All I can tell you is what I know," Anamika said, "beyond a doubt. I can't tell you how I know it. I could talk of my experience, but my experience doesn't matter to you. Is knowledge born from experience or is experience born from knowledge? Or belief? Or physiology? Or logic? It doesn't matter.

"What matters is this: you exist outside of space and time. You are not only sitting here in this room in Tiru with me, but if you listen to yourself carefully and pay attention to each little thing going on *inside* of you, you'll find that you exist in other places and times at once. That feeling, there, the one you just had when I said that. The passing thought that immediately followed. That flicker at the outskirts of your vision. The shifting patterns you see when you close your eyes. Each of these sensations is the tip of the iceberg of a fuller reality, a multi-dimensional reality. That trace of a notion that passes through you unexamined and barely noticed lives an existence in another dimension where, for example, it comes to fruition and is explored. There are indeed many 'you's,' or many aspects of a greater you, if you like—just like you have many aspects of your personality. Some aspects of your personality are latent, while others are explored. You are a microcosm. And all aspects of you are energy, and all energy goes somewhere, lives its electric-creative life, and is never destroyed.

"You can sense these other dimensions. They are here as much as the table is, the shelf, the clock. You are just more attuned to the configurations of shifting wave-particles that appear as 'solid' objects. Now even plodding scientific research has proven that solidity is an illusion, that what seems solid is fluid, ever-changing, untouchable at its core. Anyhow. You focus on these configurations easily. But at many moments throughout your day, you do focus elsewhere, just like you do when you dream at night. Or daydream. Or get lost in your imagination.

"Whenever you use your intuition, which is more often than you think, whenever you understand what someone is really saying, the meaning beneath the words, these are just the very tips of the deep, vast, multi-dimensionality of your existence. Because you don't believe in the validity of these glimpses, you shrug them off and say you spaced out, or you had a feeling, a hunch, or you thought for a minute that…oh, never mind. Then you bring your focus back to the table. (And the table is as much a symbol as the language you use for it. But I'll get to that another time, if you ever come back to see me again after today!)"

The German couple laughed politely at this. The woman looked at the table as if she were seeing it for the first time. Anamika could tell that they were listening attentively. She hoped they could understand her English well enough, for she couldn't say this any differently. It was all just coming out of her mouth without much thought, and she was letting the words fall where they may.

"When you 'die,' what simply happens is you shift focus. Nothing really changes that much. There is no loss; nothing and no one disappears."

At this point, the woman interrupted. "But how can you say this? My friend died. Katrin, she is gone now. I can't see her. I have lost her. No?" There were tears in her eyes.

Anamika spoke gently and slowly now.

"You haven't lost her; what you think you have lost is really the relationship you had with her. But that relationship *still exists*. I think you know that already. In fact, she only existed to you in your world. You made what she was to you. She was someone else to each person she encountered. They each saw her in a different way, and their perception of her became who she was to them. You can understand that, yes? So, like you, she isn't contained within one consistent, uniform reality.

"The people who are important to you are like constellations of stars in the night sky. You are part of the constellation. From another perspective, say an earthly one, you can see the light of only some stars in your constellation. What you see shifts depending on your vantage point. It doesn't mean that the stars you can't see have disappeared.

"We each exist this way to each other, flickering in and out. Death is but another flicker. The constellation remains—the relationships, which are, ultimately, a kind of love.

"You know the movie, *The Wizard of Oz*? When Dorothy in *The Wizard of Oz* completes her journey and wakes up in her bed, she looks around her and sees all the people she loved who were there with her on her adventure. The Tin Woodman, the Scarecrow, and the Cowardly Lion look like regular people now, her neighbors. They are all smiling at her from around her bed. She says, 'You were there. And you. And you!'

"When you die, you retain the connections you have with others because they are all still there. They are as much with you there as they are here because there is no 'here and there.' Like Dorothy's friends, the people may not look the same, but you recognize them. They are as much with you after death as they are in this life that you think you are in—because they exist in many dimensions at once, as do you.

"So those who welcome you to the 'other side' when you die are not just those you loved who died before you. They are just the ones you first perceive because of your belief in a 'before and after.' They are the ones you expect to do that meet-

and-greet you've heard so much about. But the truth is all of those whose lives are entwined closely with yours here are there too. They are all there!

"Here's another way to think about it: The play is over. It was your play: you wrote, directed, and starred in it. The curtain falls, the audience applauds, and you walk off the stage. You leave that play, you die, that character doesn't exist anymore. And now you're backstage with the entire cast—only nobody is in character anymore; you have all removed the costumes that you wore in that particular play. But you're all still there together, just looking a bit different, like Dorothy's friends. You're not playing that particular role to that person anymore. You have many potential characters inside of you, inside of your whole Self, your backstage self.

"One more thing: You've both heard the stories of 'near death experiences,' yes?"

The German couple nodded their heads in unison.

"And what is common to each of these experiences is the great sense of peace that the dying people say they feel. They tell us later that they didn't want to 'come back' to the life they knew because this feeling of peace was so beautiful and complete. So think about this: How could it be that people feel such incredible peace if they know that leaving their loved ones is causing those people they love horrible grief and pain and loss?"

The man spoke up. "Ah, this is a very good point you are making. I haven't heard it spoken before. No one likes making people they love feel bad. So, I think this is an important question, yes."

"Yes," Anamika replied. "It is the crux of it all. Have they, upon dying, suddenly become selfish and unaware of how others feel? Of the pain they are causing them by leaving them? Have they suddenly stopped caring? The answer is no. And why is that?"

Anamika's voice dropped to a whisper. "It is because they aren't leaving anything or anyone. The world as they knew it falls away because it only existed in their perception. No one is left behind. You're all still there, stars in a constellation, just flickering in a different way because you've shifted your perspective."

The woman spoke again. "This is now too much for me. My mind is, how you say in English. Boggling."

"Understandably," said Anamika. She added playfully, "It takes time to fully sense the illusion of time."

CHAPTER 8

O kay, so maybe D is "enlightened," or whatever you want to call it: self-realized, awake. You can feel it, something special about him. See it in the light in his eyes. Hear it in the words that fall out of his mouth like precious stones. And he talks about what it's like being this way. Enlightened. Jonas thought he might now believe in it. It's the first time Jonas heard anyone describe the…state? Stateless state? Because apparently it's not a state at all. It's simply reality. Us unrealized beings, we experience "states."

This is what Jonas learned in satsang: We live in a world of subject and object, duality, where we think we are separate from each other and the world—and that separation promotes desire and fear, both of which cause suffering. We are always either trying to get something (desire) or trying to get away from something (fear). But this world is an illusion, a dream, a fiction, a symbolic play. The more you can see through the illusory, symbolic nature of it all, the less the ego-mind has a hold, and the dream begins dissolving.

D has woken up from his dream. He isn't separate from anyone or anything because he has realized his true nature and transcended all illusions of self and other, self and world. Everything and everyone is a part of it, is inside of it, inside of him, his "Self," as D and Ramana say. Big "S" "Self." Not small "s" "self," which is just the puny, misguided, self-important ego that creates and maintains the separation. Big "S" Self is, as Jonas understands it, God, or All That Is, Source, Consciousness. Being silent and still, disassociated from the endless comings and goings of life, helps to get you there—to what is unchanging and real—and wears down the addiction to distraction, the habitual pulling of your attention into the fictional drama where you become mesmerized. That's why D starts his satsangs in meditation.

D also touched on Ramana's technique to realization, "self-inquiry." All you need to do is ask yourself, "Who am I?" Jonas has heard popular gurus in the West teach something similar. It went something like this: You talk of "my body," "my mind," "myself." But who is saying "my"? You are not the body or mind if you are referring to them in this way. You must, then, be something different from them, different from your mind, your thoughts, your body, your personality, yourself. So, who are you? Who is the "I"? Where is the "I"? Can you locate it?

D said that if you really look for it, you'll find that it's impossible to find. Looking for the "I" is like trying to see your eyes.

Jonas didn't really grasp this. Every time he tried to follow this line of thought, he ended up nowhere. It was really hard to think about, and he didn't know why. It just made no sense. Was that the point? Was this self-inquiry thing like a Zen koan, supposed to turn you inside-out and blow your mind? Make you stop thinking altogether? And thus wake you up? Maybe that was it.

D kept on saying that we can know who we really are by just feeling our own existence, our aliveness—in the body it is the heart, but it can be felt everywhere. Be still and silent and feel your heart.

"Feel your own heart. Right now. It's simple," he said. "So simple."

So Jonas stopped thinking about finding his "I" and fell into the feeling of his heart. His newly opened, airy heart. The room sank into quiet meditation and Jonas along with it, and some time must have passed because the next thing Jonas knew D was saying in his gentle voice, "Thank you all for satsang," and he walked out of the room as the people bowed to him, palms together.

A woman with white hair and a kind face stood up and told the group that this was the last public satsang with D, and if anyone was interested in a two-week retreat with him in an ashram outside of Tiru, to come and see her.

Jonas was rooted to the spot. He felt as he did when he first saw Arunachala: there was a weight deep at the base of his spine, and his spine extended down into the earth. People slowly got up and filed out of the room, and Jonas remained. His head had flopped forward onto his chest, too heavy to hold up. A small group was talking at the back of the room. The sounds flowed over Jonas like a river over a rock.

"Excuse me." A smiling woman approached him, the same woman who had spoken to the group. "Are you interested in attending the retreat?"

Without thinking, speaking from that place of stillness, Jonas heard himself reply. "Yes, I am."

He arose dreamily and followed the woman to the back of the room. There were a few others registering for the retreat; most had registered before, it seemed. Jonas discovered that the cost of the retreat was almost exactly the amount he had left in his bank account. Well, that was that then.

It would appear that Jonas had a guru. Jonas was amazed at this, but somehow it felt right. He was happy. And calm. What was that saying? "When the student is ready, the teacher appears." He guessed he must have been ready. He had seen his worst fears realized, watched all of his familiar life-structures blown apart in a terrible tornado. He had survived that.

But, really, this was a surprise. A big surprise. He'd never thought of himself as the devotee type. Yet being here in India, near this mountain, was like being on another planet. None of the old ways applied. Here it was already blown apart. There was nothing to hold on to.

Thinking of old ways… Jonas hadn't felt a poem come since he arrived in India. He wondered about that. Was his becoming D's student somehow replacing that other stuff? He kind of missed it. But what he found in D was more than he could have ever dreamed. More than his magical little poems. More than the special feeling they gave him and the wonder about where they came from. Somehow being with D was beyond all of that. It was like being in truth with a capital "T." Jonas didn't even feel flaky having these thoughts. He just felt filled with love.

Jonas hadn't been in love since Carla. And what he felt for D was truly being in love. It wasn't just that he loved him; he was in love with him. Him. A man. Jonas wasn't gay. There were no romantic-sexual feelings there. He just wanted to be with D all the time. He longed to be near him. He was happiest when he was near him. He thought about him constantly. He carried him in his heart. And Jonas didn't expect anything in return. So far, anyway. Wasn't that being in love?

He'd heard of devotees falling in love with their teachers. It was part of the process, he realized. You had to have this intense love relationship with your guru, this commitment, otherwise you weren't invested enough. You weren't ready. And the love is the door. Your master asks nothing less than all of you, and the journey you embark upon asks nothing less than everything. This is what it's all about. This is life's goal, its purpose. This is the greatest thing there is. Being here with D was the only place to be. Jonas was so sure of this, he'd bet his life on it. In a way, he already had.

II: DREAMS

(Fire)

Row, row, row your boat
Gently down the stream
Merrily, merrily, merrily, merrily
Life is but a dream

— *Traditional*

CHAPTER 9

Jonas has his own little brick-and-concrete cottage in the ashram. It's very basic: there's a wooden bed frame with the usual hard mattress, a few hooks on the walls to hang clothes, and a sink, toilet, and cold-water bucket shower. But the ashram grounds are beautiful and spacious, sprawling every which way beneath Arunachala, which is so close there is nothing between the ashram and the mountain but a farmer's field. There are about thirty cottages with pathways winding among them, some stone benches and sculptures, a lotus pond, a dining hall, and a meditation hall in the center of the grounds, home to a large intricate bas-relief of Hindu gods and goddesses on the wall behind the dais. Neither of these halls have walls so they feel airy, unlike his cottage which has a funny smell. Peacocks wander the dirt ground outside his cottage, and inside, geckos wander the walls. The peacocks meow and the geckos chirp. What a strange world this is.

Jonas can't help but wonder if this "letting the mind go" is really a falling into a dream. Rather than waking up. He stands inside his cottage: no thought, empty head, clear mind. Nothing to do. So he unpacks his pack, hangs up some clothes on the hooks in the wall, puts his toothbrush on the sink. Notices the gecko shit everywhere. Finds his travel cup, puts his toothbrush in that. Looks at himself in the mirror above the sink. Stubble on his jaw and chin. Long nose. Long face.

Long hair. Is that a new mole on his chin? He already has many of those, forming a constellation on his left cheek.

His father always told him to use his mind and talents to give back to the world, to contribute to society. It was his obligation as a gifted person. So why should he seek to leave himself? Leave his mind behind? Leave the world behind? Isn't this just being selfish? Or is living in your true Self the most selfless way? There was an irony there somewhere. Or a paradox. Everything important seemed to be a paradox when you got right down to the bones of it.

Thoughts keep rushing in. Do others have the same questions? Jonas can't ask them because the retreat is supposed to be silent. No talking unless necessary. He wouldn't know how to ask, anyway. What—you just go right up to someone you don't know and say, hey, so isn't it better doing good in the world than sitting around meditating all the time? Maybe he should ask D in satsang. That's where people can talk—to D that is, if they feel "pulled" to "take the chair" next to him and be with him, in front of the gathered group of devotees, the sangha. But he'd feel stupid asking such a question. He's pretty sure everyone else already knows the answer.

The retreat officially begins tomorrow. Two weeks of this. What has he gotten himself into? Jonas suddenly feels confused. He has doubts. They keep multiplying. He takes a deep breath and walks out of his cottage to where he can see the mountain. He checks his watch: one hour to dinner. Enough time for a walk. So he lets himself be drawn closer to the mountain, finds a path and walks it.

He passes by what seems to be a deep stone well, and peers in. Fleeting vertigo. A funny feeling in his knees. What if he fell in? Would anyone find him? Would he drown down there? He lets himself imagine falling falling falling. He feels panic lurch in his stomach, desperation constrict his lungs. He imagines falling falling falling…until he feels no fear. Further on down the path, just before the field, he comes upon a house and is surprised to see a woman from the ashram walk up the outside stairway that ascends to the roof. Jonas follows her. The rooftop patio is tiled and spacious, and there are a few people from the ashram there—mostly meditating with eyes closed, some in yoga poses, one reading a book with Ramana's image on the cover. They are all facing the same direction, toward the mountain. Jonas finds a spot on the roof and sits in a half-lotus and closes his eyes.

When he opens them, everyone has gone and the light is fading. How long has it been? Where has he been? How did he not hear everyone leave? Jonas turns his gaze to the mountain, wondering what just happened. Arunachala has what looks like thin streaks of black on its rock face, lines that fall like water. Maybe they were left behind from the last monsoon, streaks of mud and dirt, or maybe they are crevices in the rock. As Jonas looks at the mountain, he can't believe what he sees. There on the face of Arunachala is his name written in the black lines in capital, if crooked, letters, as clear as can be: JONAS. Jonas stares at it for a long time.

Okay. You got me.

After the vegetarian dinner served buffet style (which Jonas was late for) he retires to his cottage, full now, filled with a sense of certainty that he is where he should be. And a poem comes. The first one in India. He feels that odd, familiar sense of himself receding into the background and images and words arising in the foreground, and grabs his pen, opens his journal.

Backwards dropping fast
Into the flying dark
The vortex swirls
And takes you into its center

How many times you have been here before
Is uncertain, uncountable
In a dream, a sleep, a moment
In the dappled sun

Is there something to find
In the movement, something to still
In a heartbeat?
What we call death is this
Finding and stilling
It is also what we call a dream
A moment of letting go
And falling, flying

Peer down into the well at my feet
You felt yourself fall in
And then I called you to me
By shaping your name on my side
A temporary tattoo
To be washed off
In the next monsoon rain

I am as much you as I am me

~

There are two satsangs each day: one in the morning, another in the afternoon. Each time, the sangha—about thirty people of varying ages, and a good mix of men and women—gathers in the meditation hall and sits together in silence for an hour and a half, then D arrives, sits in his chair on the dais, and gives a monologue, after which the floor is open for questions and comments. There is an empty chair beside D, for those who want to come up and ask a question.

Jonas loves the sitting part. He finds he can drop into himself easily, like a pebble in a well, down into the silence. Sometimes he has thoughts; sometimes, emotions. But rarely does he get himself all tangled up inside. Probably his earlier forays into meditation help, back when he was taking Eastern Religious Studies courses at university and yoga classes at the community center, and learning how to meditate. Not having thoughts feels like an escape from himself, and that is sweet relief. He doesn't always have to be himself. Whew.

And he really *really* loves the monologue-dialogue part. This morning, it seemed to Jonas that D held his eyes deeply before he began to talk.

"Welcome," says D, smiling warmly at the sangha. "Today I'd like to speak about where my words come from." D's soft, quiet voice seems to fill the entire meditation hall.

"The words that come out of this body don't come from a mind, an ego. They come from no one, not someone. They are received and then given, one word after another. There is sound, there is vibration in this chest. But there is no doer here. Where there is no 'I,' there is no doer. There is only one thing, and that is the Self. That is where the words come from. They come from you." D leans forward a little, toward us.

"For this one," D taps his chest, "the illusion of doing is gone. You are not doing either; you only think you are. The ego likes to think it has control. But in truth it has no control. Everything that is in your life is being divinely orchestrated. It is perfect. And the more you surrender to the silence within you, the more apparent this is. It all falls into place. In the not-doing, it all gets done.

"You know nothing. You think you know, but you don't." D smiles and leans back in his chair. "This is another illusion that the ego-mind maintains. Knowing and doing are the same—they are two sides to the same coin, which disappears if you move your glance away. The coin disappears because it was never real in the first place." D rubs his fingers together and then lets them go with a flourish, as if he were a magician doing a disappearing-coin trick.

"If you surrender to not-knowing, you are giving in to truth, to what is. Trust in knowing nothing. For therein lies true humility, and in true humility lies the opening to your Self. In knowing nothing, you know everything."

D closes his eyes briefly. When he opens them again, he looks around the room lovingly, like we are all his family. "The floor is open for your questions." He nods at one young man with a topknot of hair, and he makes his way to the chair beside D on the dais.

He sits quietly in the chair and he and D just look into each other's eyes for a while. Then they both laugh.

"Hi, Brahma." D exudes warmth to the young American man with the god's name, and takes his hand.

"D, I'm having my usual mental contortions over doing things in the world. I feel I should have a career, go to school, do something with my life. I wonder if I am being selfish pursuing just…this, with you. I know, you've heard all this from me before."

Jonas inhales quickly, recognizing his recent question in Brahma's.

"Brahma," D's eyes remain locked with his. "Tell me: Where is the world?"

Brahma looks around him. "Here!" He smiles, and many of the sangha laugh.

"I'm sorry. Where? Where is 'the world' right *now*?" Brahma has no answer.

They sit, continuing to hold each other's eyes for a good minute, until they both laugh and hug. Brahma lays his forehead briefly on D's knee, and D strokes his head. As he walks back to his seat, his face is relaxed and shining.

After lunch, there are a couple of hours until the next satsang begins. Jonas is beginning to understand that most of the people here know each other from the States. They all live together in a community somewhere with D himself, and they all come here, to India, to the holy mountain of Arunachala to go on a special retreat. Jonas realizes he is one of the newbies here, like the three who registered with him in town at the last public satsang. This alters the way Jonas sees the interactions between D and the people of the sangha. No wonder he knows their

names, and there is a familiarity with them. Jonas feels a twinge of jealousy. He
wants D to know him that way, too.

After Brahma took the chair in the morning satsang, a few others followed—
all of whom knew D, and he, them. D was like a father to some, a husband to
others. It seemed that everyone knew him in their own unique ways; each person
in the sangha had a different relationship with him. But all of these relationships
were close, very close. It all looked like love. Indeed, some told D they loved him.
Most of the time he said the same words back.

This love, this history they share—Jonas feels like an outsider who wants to
be part of the "in" crowd. It's not because of how he's treated: everyone has been
very welcoming to him. They smile at him. He's even received some hugs. But he
longs for the intimacy they have with D. He wants it so much he can taste it.

Jonas wonders if the other newbies feel the same way. He remembers
something D said in a public satsang, that everyone sees him differently. Because
he is no one, he becomes whatever you need him to be. He appears differently to
each person because each person projects their own stuff onto him, the stuff they
need to see so that they can burn through it. He's like a still, clear pond in which
we see our own reflection. He is, ultimately, us. Jonas recalls the words D spoke
to a man in a public satsang: "This body is here, that body is there. But the taste
is the same."

In the afternoon satsang, after the "sitting," there is no monologue. Rather D
opens the floor right away. Jonas is determined to take the chair beside him, to
start a relationship with D. But at the same time he is afraid. What if D isn't loving
toward him?

Hands go up. One by one, people take the chair beside D on the dais. Jonas
puts up his hand tentatively. D doesn't see him. What if he never sees me? Jonas
feels like a little boy again, trying to get his father's attention. Look at me, Daddy!
Watch me go down the slide!

In the playground, his father is talking to a pretty young woman by the swing
set. Four-year-old Jonas gets his courage up and goes down the slide. He feels

proud of himself. When he reaches the bottom, he looks hopefully at his father who is still engrossed in conversation, laughing with the young mother. He didn't see him. Jonas bursts into tears. Finally his father notices him and comes over, squats down beside him.

"Was that scary, son? Did the slide scare you?" Jonas cries harder. His father looks around, embarrassed.

D announces that there is time for just one more person. Jonas's hand shoots up. D sees him, and nods.

Jonas's heart races as he walks to the dais. Before he reaches it, he looks behind him at the sangha. Most people have their eyes closed. He feels comforted by that. He sits in the chair and looks into D's eyes. And starts to cry.

Jonas glances at D through his tears, and D's eyes gaze kindly at him, which makes him cry harder. D leans over and puts his arms around Jonas and holds him tight. The only sound he hears is his own sobbing. After what seems like a long time, the sound subsides. He pulls himself out of D's hug and looks into his eyes.

D smiles and asks him his name.

"Jonas."

"Jonas. Welcome. How are you?"

Jonas feels a warm wave flowing right over his body, as if he were lying on the soft sand of a tropical beach, letting the waves wash over him. Whatever pain he was experiencing has evaporated. He feels comfortable, easy.

"I'm good, D. I'm happy to be here."

D laughs at this, and takes his hand. "I'm happy you're here."

Jonas sinks into this warmth, and just sits quietly for a while, looking right into D's eyes. There's nowhere else he can look. He's never seen eyes like his before. They go in forever. And they don't seem to blink.

"This longing you are experiencing is the longing for your Self, you know. Nothing more or less."

The image of Jonas's name on the side of the mountain rises up within him, and he tells D about the vision. It feels like it's just Jonas and D talking together, all by themselves. It feels like he can tell him anything.

D's face is serious as he talks to Jonas. "How very beautiful. What grace."

D pauses and his gaze intensifies. "You know, Jonas, it's all symbolic. Everything you see around you is a symbol. The so-called world is really your mirror, reflecting you and showing you what you need to know about yourself. Everything that you see, that comes up, is there just for you. It is there, ultimately, to bring you home. To bring you back to your Self. Which you never really left."

Another pause. "What does your name on the mountain mean to you?"

Jonas has no idea. He just holds D's eyes. Words fall out of his mouth into the air.

"The mountain told me, 'I am as much you as I am me.' It means we are one and the same."

"Yes," D nods his head solemnly. "And the mountain is God."

Jonas and D hold eyes for a few seconds longer, then D tilts his head to one side, smiles, and puts his palms together in Namaste. Jonas feels very humbled to receive Namaste from D. He returns the gesture with all of his heart. Even so he feels it's not enough.

"Thank you, D."

"You are most welcome."

Jonas feels so light as he returns to his seat that he doesn't know if his feet are touching the ground.

CHAPTER 10

Anamika dreams that she is flying over Arunachala. It's the time of year when the Indians light an enormous vat of ghee on the top of the mountain in honor of Shiva, and the flames reach far into the sky. From where she is soaring very high above the mountain, the fire glows red-orange like embers in a campfire, and as she looks down she feels herself being drawn to it. She begins to fall. At first she is frightened, and then she gives in. She can feel the heat intensify as she falls closer, getting hotter and hotter, the flames growing huge, until she is in the fire and all she can see is bright white light surrounding her.

Anamika wakes up hot in the sunshine pouring in her window, and kicks her sheet off. A few days have passed since the German couple came over. Anamika wonders if she scared them off. The people, the dogs, the crows, the cow...they have all disappeared from her front stoop. Anamika doesn't mind. She has worked her two days at Ramu's agency, mainly helping customers use the internet that Ramu offers in an adjoining room, and occasionally helping Ramu explain the intricacies of train tickets. She is beginning to enjoy the conversations she hears around her, and occasionally participates in them.

What she likes about these spiritual tourists is that they are all looking for something beyond their day-to-day physical existence, and many of them have experienced something more. Some of them are true "seekers," and she appreciates that. Just like she appreciated the German couple who graced her little room that day. These people come from all over the world to be close to this mountain. They were drawn here, like she was. Some of them call Arunachala the center of the world. Some of them speak of Ramana Maharshi as if he were God. All Anamika knows is that she is here, and she isn't going to leave anytime soon. That's something that comes up a lot, too. How many people just can't leave this place. It is as if there were a powerful magnet holding them here. The magnet mountain. Filled with iron ore. Arunachala goes by many names, but literally speaking, the word in Sanskrit means the "sacred red mountain."

Anamika boils an egg in a pot on her hot plate and eats it with naan. She feels like a cup of chai from the stall down the street, and ventures outside. As she walks down the dusty road she feels light, as if her feet are barely touching the ground. When she returns to her place, there is a small group of people outside. The German couple is there, as well as a muscular blond man in shorts and an orange Aum t-shirt, a petite, olive-skinned woman in a turquoise salwar kameez, and a middle-aged Indian woman in a faded yellow sari, with rows of blue and gold sparkly bangles hugging her forearms.

As she approaches, the German couple smiles broadly at her, and everyone gestures Namaste. Anamika returns the greeting and invites them inside. The blond man presents her with a box of sweets. Anamika peeks inside: barfi, her favorite! She thanks him, and he bows his head in response.

They gather in a little half-circle on the floor, and silently wait. The Germans close their eyes. Anamika draws up a chair in front of the little gathering, sips her chai, and also waits.

The blond man speaks with a Canadian accent. "What shall we call you, Guruji?"

Anamika briefly wonders at being addressed as a guru, and closes her eyes to let it sink in. When she opens them, she looks with all of her senses into the eyes of each person there, one by one, and is satisfied. "You can call me Anamika," she says.

The Indian woman's words come out in a breath. "No name!"

Anamika begins to speak, letting the words fall out.

"Everything in your life, every person, thing, event, is part of your movie or, if you like, your novel. You know very well that your life is unique, and how you look at life is unique. Even people who are very close to each other for years, who share everything, know that their perspective and thus their world is entirely different from the person's they are close to. You know, too, that each person witnessing the same event, say a collision between a street dog and a rickshaw, sees it differently. As much as we might want to know each other's world, we can't. Each of us truly lives in a separate world.

"We make sense of our world by creating a kind of narrative about it through interpreting the events, people, and things, so that there exists a kind of coherency, a narrative thread, and in turn, a way of explaining our interpretation, our version of the story, to others.

"When your high school English teacher asked you to interpret a short story, she was not asking what the story really means, what it's really about, but for you to create a reasoned interpretation of it, taking into account its symbols and metaphors, theme, plot, characters, and so on. There are no real answers to meaning, though students seek them anyway. There is no 'whole story.' We are, each of us, interpreters of what we imagine we perceive outside of ourselves. The interpretation reflects ourselves back to us, and in this way it is a circular creative process. Because your narrative is so coherent and tightly woven, you see your interpretation of events *justified* everywhere you look. But it's really you doing everything. We are creating our lives, our world, in the same way that when we interpret a short story we are creating another text.

"Everything is symbolic, metaphorical, and the meaning of the symbol lies within you. Interpret it. There is a message there for you. If your life were a movie or novel, how would you describe its main theme? Its secondary theme? What repeats in your life; what do you see happening again and again? If your life were a movie, what would be the opening scene?"

Anamika begins to feel a burning inside. She closes her eyes. When she opens them, she sees the people gathered as if they are children, in school, paying attention to their teacher. She knows what to do. She excuses herself and finds some paper and a few pencils.

"I want you to do this exercise now, if you're up for it," she says as she hands out the paper and pencils. "First, close your eyes. Imagine that a friend of yours wants to watch a movie, and selects one that has your name in the title. You've clicked Play. The movie opens. What is the first scene? Write it or draw it on the paper. Don't think about it. Just do it."

The group shifts about, and the petite woman raises her hand.

Anamika says that she won't take questions. There is no wrong way to do this. "I'm giving you ten minutes for this," she says. The work begins. After ten minutes is over, Anamika gives another instruction. "Those of you who wrote about the scene, I want you now to draw it, and vice versa. Ten minutes!"

The group is especially engaged with this second exercise. Whereas the first exercise took a couple of them a while to get going on, they are all completely engaged with writing and drawing now. When Anamika announces the ten minutes are over, a few keep working, unaware she has spoken.

"Finally, I want you to give your movie a title. Remember: It has your name in it! Two minutes for this."

The people seem to want to share their opening scenes and titles with each other, and are already doing this—showing their drawings, reading their writing aloud. Anamika just watches them. They huddle together as if they are keeping warm over a fire. There is a heat in the air, passion, emotions sparking and falling. Self-discoveries are being made.

When the creative fire turns to embers, Anamika is ready to close the session. "Let's just breathe together for a while. If it helps, breathe in 'here,' and breathe out 'now.'" Their breathing is at first noisy, then quiets down. She can hear some soft intakes of the word "here," and the breathing out of the word "now." When she senses calm in the room and feels the air cooling, Anamika thanks them all for coming to visit her.

"When may we come again, Anamikaji?" the blond man asks. They arrange to come back the day after next. On the way out, he stops to talk with her. His name is Bruce, and he is also from Vancouver.

After he leaves, Anamika hops on her scooter and drives into town to shop for more pencils, pens, and paper.

CHAPTER 11

Jonas finds that life in the retreat has taken on a dream-like quality. It has become transparent; he can almost see through it. What he sees around him and feels within him are phenomena arising as out of a dream, a living, fluctuating piece of multi-dimensional art, rich in symbol and metaphor, that morphs as he moves through it.

The satsangs—the long meditations, D's talks—are taking root within him. D's words seem to come from inside Jonas. They live at the base of his spine and, when D speaks them, they move through him as his own breath. And settle in his heart.

Jonas recalls that D said in a recent monologue that to be awake, or enlightened, means awaking from the dream of life. When we are sleeping and dreaming, we are usually completely immersed in our dreams and don't know we are sleeping or dreaming. Then, when we wake up, we see our dreams from a different perspective, as a witness. And we see how everything that occurred in our dream was symbolic; we perhaps interpret the meaning of our dream. And we may see that the other people in our dream were just aspects of ourselves, because it is only our dream.

In other words, it's only me. When I dream, the dreams are all about me, and I am everything and everyone in my dream. How can it be otherwise? I am the only dreamer of these dreams. That's what I find when I wake up. But I don't know all this when I am asleep and in a dream. Except in rare moments of lucidity.

Jonas sees how it's exactly the same in his life, in the world. It's all him, just him. And how, when he finally awakes—and he has moments of lucidity now, has experienced openings—he will be everything he sees in the world and everyone he meets.

~

When Jonas wakes at 5:30 AM, he doesn't join his fellow sangha members for chai in the dining hall and a dawn walk to the mountain, as he usually does. He has had a dream. And he feels he needs to write something. He feels this need urgently. Because he has been instructed to do so. And Jonas was always a good student—he was in university for many years, after all—and he was a pretty good teacher of college English, too.

In his dream, Jonas was reading a book that had his name in the title. And he was reading these words while, at the same time, hearing them—in a woman's voice that somehow seemed familiar:

"You read books. I know, because you're reading this one. When you read, say, a novel, you know it's not the 'real world.' If it's good, you might get lost in it, suspend your belief for the sake of the experience. It becomes real to you, in a way. And reading the good novel becomes another experience that is yours, and that you can share with others who have read the same book.

"Just for a minute, imagine that your life, your world, is like a book you're reading. A good book. So good that you may have already forgotten that you're imagining it all. You've suspended your belief for the sake of the experience. You may indeed believe that it's the real world. And that's okay, especially if you're having a good time in it.

"You are the main character, the protagonist, of course. Look around you. Those objects, that person, even that tree, are there for a reason—to create an atmosphere, support the plot, lay the framework for action, draw a scene. Look at your hands that hold this book; they are shaped a certain way, beautifully drawn, unique to you. You have expressed the shape of your hands, your body, the features of your face, just as you have expressed everything you see, every situation you're in. It's an intimate and ongoing art project, and that hand you see is in everything.

"Just for the heck of it, put this book down for a minute. And close your eyes.

"Oh, hi. Welcome back. Okay, here's a little writing activity for you. Give yourself five minutes for each part, and don't stop writing. Don't worry; no one will judge you. No one will even read it but you. This is for you. Just you.

1. How would you describe the scene you're in now? Don't forget to pay attention to mood and atmosphere.
2. If your novel-life had three major themes, what would they be?
3. What are the three main struggles of the protagonist?"

Jonas writes for fifteen minutes. Then he keeps on writing. It comes quickly and easily, and it comes from him, not from another mysterious source. He feels something burning inside him, as if he is burning away old stuff that he doesn't need to keep anymore. It feels good. Creative. Passionate. Alive. Emotions spark and fall.

At the morning satsang, when he drops into meditation, flickers of thoughts filter down like wavering ribbons of light from the surface, down into the depths of his pool.

Either there is something out there, or it's all in here and reflected out there. The world mirroring our own inner landscape, allowing us to meet what we need to. The world as symbol, metaphor, always personally meaningful if you can see it, if you can understand, interpret the symbols.

He feels he is starting again somehow. He is at the beginning of his book.

III: RELATIONSHIPS

(Sound)

From Om, the soundless roar!
From Om, the call for light o'er dark to roam.
From Om the music of the spheres!
From Om the mist of nature's tears!
All things of earth and heaven declare, Om!
Om! Resounding everywhere!

— Paramahansa Yogananda

CHAPTER 12

Anamika had given another session, and more people had come. At the beginning of that last session, Sita, the middle-aged Indian woman, quietly confided in Anamika that she had discovered a lot about herself through the "opening scene" activity. The petite woman, Maryam, said that it was a refreshing change to actually do something other than just sit in a satsang.

There was that word: *satsang*. Anamika didn't realize she was giving satsang, literally a "meeting with truth," but perhaps she was. To her, she was just someone talking about what she knows, and she gave an activity to help those listening to really understand it—to learn it by doing, by letting it come out of themselves, by allowing their bodies to absorb it as it moved through them. Anamika hadn't noticed it before, but maybe her mother did indeed pass down her teaching abilities, along with the actress ones. It seems like she has a knack for it. And it seems that she truly is a guru, a teacher, giving satsang.

Last satsang's monologue followed from the one before, and went like this:

"Just as no one is left behind after you die, so too can you leave nothing behind after death. People work so hard to leave a legacy for their children, to leave a mark upon the world, to be remembered by future generations as having done something worthwhile in their lifetime. Isn't that what so many of us are trying to do? Make the world a better place for our being here? Make our mark upon it? Isn't that also what brings people shame and feelings of failure—when they feel useless, of no value to society? When they aren't affecting others?

"By the way, on another level: You can never know how you affect people. How you *think* you affect them—which you glean from what they say about you and their reactions to you, for example—is usually not the reality of it. The reality is that you touch people all the time in ways you have no idea about. The number of people at your funeral is no indicator of your effect either. Famous people don't touch more people; they just have different kinds of effects. Even your smallest, most inconsequential action has far-reaching and unimaginable effects and implications that ripple out from it, like the circular waves around a pebble tossed into a lake.

"Okay, back to the larger level: You very well are asking yourself, What does she mean there is no legacy left behind? What about photographs? What about what I leave in my will? I have grandma's diamond ring. I have a whole attic filled with Mom and Dad's and Uncle Bob's stuff. And then there are the family trees, museums and archives, history books, art galleries, and on and on…What crazy shit is she telling us now?

"It's pretty crazy shit. But it's true. All of the world, including its histories, its made-up stories, exists in your perception. Just like how the people in your world exist only in relationship *to you*, so does the world exist only in relationship *to you*. And when you die, it disappears, having had no separate, independent existence. It disappears along with your legacy—which was really only important *to you*, something you did for yourself because you needed to, like you do everything."

She led them in a guided meditation to help bring the content of her talk home. She called it her "Just me" meditation. After that, the group, as expressed by those who had attended her previous satsang, wanted to continue working on interpreting their lives through creative exercises. So Anamika had them describe the scene they were currently in and their three main life-themes and struggles, all through writing.

Today the group is so large, they barely fit comfortably in her room. The German couple, Kris and Gabi, as well as Bruce, Sita, and Maryam, whom together Anamika thinks of as "the original five," are always the first to arrive. Anamika often begins as she does now, with a guided meditation where she brings the attention up through the body, from the soles of the feet to the top of the head, pausing where there is discomfort and observing what is there. Then they just sit and breathe together, sometimes using her "here, now" mantra, until Anamika knows that everyone is fully present and undistracted. Then she usually begins her talk. Today, however, Bruce has his hand raised.

"May I ask a question, Anamikaji?"

"Sure, Bruce." She has been learning some names, though some are unusual and don't fix in her mind. Bruce's does though. His was the first name she learned, and besides, he's from her hometown.

"What about reincarnation? Can you talk about that please?"

"The stumbling block is in that pesky prefix in 'reincarnation.' I'm talking about the 're.'" She pauses here. The words aren't coming as easily as before; they aren't just falling out of her mouth. She takes a deep breath.

She must go slowly when she talks about language and time. She knows her own language can be dense and perhaps difficult at times, but she doesn't know how else to say this kind of stuff. She just has to trust that understanding will be reached somehow. At least here, she thinks (she hopes), she won't be the object of ridicule or rage as she was back home, the odd (and usually drunken) time she decided to speak the truth. So she continues, as clearly as she can. She feels as if she's unraveling a huge, ornate tapestry, one color-soaked thread at a time.

Since she already spoke before about the illusion of time, she goes from there.

"In this case, the belief in time—or, if you like, linear time—causes the trouble. 'Re' means 'again.' 'Reincarnate' is to 'incarnate again.' 'Again' implies a before and after, a line of moments extending backwards and forwards, like this line of ants moving across my wall from that window to the shelf." Anamika points to the ants. A few people laugh. She has tried to coax them out of her room, but, well, this is India.

"Everything is here and now. You exist now only. You don't exist in the past or future. This is simple logic. So, too, you are never somewhere other than right here. Again, logical-seeming, right? And also paradoxical, like all truths are when words are used to express them, because words are caught in time. Time is an illusion that we all buy into. A convention, if you prefer. I know this is difficult to understand, but if you can only catch a glimpse of this, a little whiff, it will be enough.

"Words, too, are like a line of ants, one following the other, maintaining the illusion of time, of going somewhere. Words also reinforce collective beliefs and assumptions. Language is metaphorical in the same way the physical world is, except language is more obviously malleable."

A woman sitting right in front of Anamika turns her gaze to the line of ants. A few people behind her follow the turn of her head.

"I have spoken before about how you are a microcosm: each aspect of your personality lives another life, fulfilling and exploring potentials that you have chosen not to in this life. These different lives exist all *at once*, simultaneously. And they are all a part of your whole Self. Look at your hand. Your hand includes your fingers; you can't tell exactly where your finger ends and your hand begins. They are all one entity. And yet, each finger moves separately, on its own, has its own function. But they exist all together. Think of each finger as another life, separate, moving on its own, yet part of the same whole Self or hand."

Anamika stretches her fingers and moves them through the air.

"Now, some lives don't even know the conditions of time and space as you do; they operate in environments quite foreign to you. What you take for granted as facts of life, like time and space, don't even exist elsewhere, in other dimensions of being. Facts are only assumptions that are collectively agreed upon. This, of course, is what makes cultures distinct, too—their agreed-upon beliefs and assumptions about the world and the way things are, which are seen as facts to the culture's inhabitants, and from which arise customs and mores that reinforce the culture's perspective."

Here a young man with an American accent interrupts with a comment. "America has a reputation for thinking its facts are every other culture's facts, too. And if other countries don't see it like us, they should! Or else! There's a word for this, isn't there?"

"Ethnocentrism!" someone pipes up. "Egotism!" suggests another. Some people laugh and others nod their heads thoughtfully.

"Aha! Yes! Thanks for that. So. Just as America may be unaware that there are other countries or cultures that see things very differently, there are vast dimensions of existence that you are mostly unaware of because you, too, sift reality through the template screen of your assumptions." Anamika separates the fingers of her hand and makes a movement as if she is sifting sand through them, and then she brings her open hand to her face, in front of her eyes, and peers through her fingers.

"For example, you may be unaware of the electro-magnetic particles in this room, the play of light on dust motes, the sounds of the street and in the breath of the person next to you, the color of the auras around bodies, the geckos on the ceiling," she speaks through her hand, then drops it into her lap. "All of this is happening right here and now, and each of these has a reality separate to you, yet also shared. So, too, are your other lives. Here and now, separate and shared. Only they usually aren't as visible as geckos! Not to most people, anyway.

"Some choose to have more lives than others. Some focus strongly in this physical time-space dimension, while others focus in dimensions not organized in the same way. The interplay of musical notes and harmonics, for example, form as cohesive a context or environment as time and space do for you here. Cool, huh. We may be emotionally moved by music, but in another dimension it actually moves and shapes matter. We may not make much use of sound's vibrational properties to heal our bodies, though we use sound and music to heal our hearts. If you have an affinity for music, say, you might be able to access this dimension of sound with a shift of focus, a turning of attention away from the physical and a tuning of the attention to another frequency. You are a microcosm of a vast universe of living swirling planets. Listen carefully." Anamika cocks her head. "Can you hear the music of the spheres?

"Everything exists now. And all of your expressions of your self, your whole Self, exist now. You will not *re*incarnate; you already have incarnations. And there is constant interplay between them and you. If you are a musician and playing your guitar, the notes that charge the air with sound play in another environment, too, though the notes vibrate in a different kind of way. You are huge, multi-dimensional, timeless, and endlessly creative.

"You are like a multi-faceted crystal hanging from the ceiling, turning this way and that, catching the light on one face, then on another. The personality you know as yourself is one face of the crystal, your partner selves are other faces. But you, your whole Self, is the entire crystal, swinging in the air. And even more: as the crystal turns and the light hits a face, it casts little dancing rainbows all over the room!"

Anamika stops talking and looks around the room. She senses a shift in the air, a need.

"Okay, I know that some of you wonder about your other lives (notice I didn't say 'past lives'!), and much is made of this in paranormal circles: 'Discover your past lives! Find out which great person in history you were!'

"Cleopatra!" a woman chimes in. Titters follow.

"Yeah. It's not hard to tune into your other lives—though some are easier to find than others, like those who share this physical dimension but are only in different 'time' periods. And that's what everyone is talking about anyway, 'past lives.' As if time only leads up to now. As I've mentioned before, you often do connect with your partner selves in your dreams and other moments when you are in an altered state of consciousness, which happens frequently enough, although it usually goes unnoticed.

"For some, the connection with a partner self can be somewhat valuable. Personally, I don't care so much about the daily lives, loves, and careers of my partner selves. Why? Because I already know the important stuff about them, because their important stuff is also mine on other levels.

"I'll give you an exercise, if you like, that will help you connect to a partner self—but I offer it mainly because it will also help you tap into the fullness of your lives and how you truly live unbounded by time and space."

A couple of hands fly up.

"I'll answer your questions later. Bruce, will you help me distribute paper and pencils?"

∽

"Hold your pencil loosely in your hand. Keep the paper beneath it or nearby." Anamika is now speaking very slowly and softly, pausing often. She is completely present in each word. "Now close your eyes, and sit any way that feels comfortable. Let your thoughts leave your mind. Don't push them out—just let them go. There is nothing at all that needs your attention right now. Nothing. There's nothing to do, nothing to remember, nothing to think about. If a thought enters, tell it you'll deal with it later. Clear a space. A wide, empty, peaceful space. Let's just sit for a while in it."

Five minutes or so pass.

"Someone is now coming into the space. Can you feel the presence, maybe see them? Feel comfortable. There's nothing to fear. In a real way, it's just you.

"Put your pencil on the paper. Don't think. If a word or image comes, write it down. Just follow it wherever it takes you, one word or image at a time. Don't anticipate. Don't do anything yourself. Don't try."

Some pencils move quickly; others don't move at all. Some people look around; others sit still with closed eyes.

After the exercise has come to a natural end, Anamika closes the session, inviting those who want to ask her questions to stay. They have a ten-minute break, and some people roam outside and chat; some do yoga stretches. Most return.

~

The first question comes from a thin grey-haired man sitting and leaning against the far wall of her room. "This is most interesting to me. I, how do you say, hold back the judging. For right now." He smiles and his face creases around his mouth and eyes. "But to ask this: Can there be more than one self incarnated in the same time span?"

"Yes, sometimes this happens when there is an affinity for a particular kind of environment. Sometimes the selves know each other. This is where the idea of 'soul mates' comes from."

The man offers another crinkly smile and thanks Anamika.

"What about future selves?" asks a woman to Anamika's right.

"Yup. You got it. Your partner selves exist in what you see as the past as well as what you think of as the future. In this physical dimension. See, without the restrictions of time, 'past' and 'future' are just meaningless categories. But, I should add, the future selves can be more difficult for you to connect with."

"Anamika?" asks a man to Anamika's left. "I take it that you time travel in a way, right?"

Anamika chuckles. "Yeah, in a sense, I guess."

"Okay. So, what about space travel? Can you talk about that?"

"I'll certainly try," Anamika responds. "Like time, space isn't what we think either. Time and space are interconnected: one doesn't exist without the other. Physics is still wrestling with space-time, of course—not that I know a lot about what's going on in that field. What I do know, and what science hasn't seen yet, is that what we call 'outer space,' with its population of planets and stars and perhaps other life, doesn't really exist. Not even in the way we think tables and chairs exist. Outer space is more 'inner space.' It's inner space turned inside out.

"Planets and stars don't have a physical reality or quality; they aren't places that we can travel to, except in a highly superficial way. They are configurations of intensely concentrated energy, like thoughts and beliefs are. Our romantic notions of stars—we wish upon them, and sing about them in songs, write about them in poetry, we connect them with our dreams and magic and showing us the way in our own lives through astrology—these are closer to the reality of what they are.

"There will be no successful space missions to other planets because they don't exist that way. Why? Because other planets are really more like those other dimensions I talk about. That's the thing. They aren't light years, galaxies away. They aren't 'away' at all. We will only travel in outer space when we learn to travel in our inner space. And we don't need to build rockets for that."

"Oh no!" someone else says, laughing. "So you're saying *Star Trek* isn't real?"

"Actually, I'm saying that it *is* real. It's just the idea of outer space that's the problem. Imagine all the *Trek* characters as aspects of the same person—Captain Kirk is the part that takes risks, Spock is the rational part, and so on—and the explorations and battles as taking place in the world of one individual. 'To boldly go,' indeed! Let's explore new worlds. They exist right here and now, inside each of us. Exciting, huh.

"*Star Trek* is an allegory, metaphorical, like all of those very special stories that come along once in a while and take hold in the minds of millions and become embedded in culture. They are collectively imagined and upheld. You know the ones I'm talking about. They are like stars, shining in the night sky, pointing the way to what we know is true in the deepest parts of ourselves.

"And on another level, maybe space *is* 'the final frontier': maybe, through our fascination with outer space, scientists will indeed get closer to the truth of it all—as close as they are able to get, anyway, with their need for quantifiable proof. And perhaps how we constantly create our reality from the inside out will become more widely understood and accepted. Neuroscience is indeed revealing how the external world is like a hologram that we project from inside our brains. And non-dualism and neuroscience are even being discussed in tandem. Perhaps we have already begun our scientific travel into inner space, the real final frontier!"

Another question comes from a man sitting right in front of her: "Back to all of the selves, if you don't mind. Not that I'm not a sci-fi fan. But, as a spiritual seeker in India, I have to ask: Is your whole self, or the whole crystal or whatever, like Ramana's Self?

"I'm not sure, but I don't think so. Ramana's Self is all that is, is God, is the indivisible unity that is also called pure love, bliss, nirvana, moksha. Perhaps it is beyond dimensional existence and experience. I don't know about that myself, except to say that if it is accessible, I can't take you there. 'Enlightenment' doesn't concern me. For that, you will need to find a master and sit at his feet."

CHAPTER 13

Jonas has gone to sleep early, as he usually does on retreat, but wakes with a start. The time on his travel clock reads 11:11 PM. He feels an urgency to write, and it comes from that place where he himself takes a back seat, where the poems came from.

Call him Joseph, the carpenter who lives in a sawdusty hut in a field with a stream not far. The air is cool in Europe, the Balkans, and his wife died of a lung ailment. Two children, Lars and Peder, help with the chores, and Peder wants to apprentice with his father. Lars has his eye on the horizon. There is a stalwart, stoic quality to their life, punctuated by moments of joy and laughter.

One day, Joseph was at work carving and hammering, constructing a cradle for a woman expecting a child in the next town. As he worked, he sang softly to himself. Lars was walking past the door of his father's work shed and heard the song, and it set a fire in his belly—the melody, the way the notes plunged and soared, the crooked catch in the chorus that made his heart beat. Lars had that melody on his mind for the next day and the next, but he wouldn't ask his father to sing it again. He wanted to keep the song for himself, wanted to know it for himself alone.

Years later when Lars was a successful, widely known, and admired luthier, he was asked how he came to learn the trade. He told the story of hearing a tune and having no means to play it himself. But having grown up with wood, he was drawn to make an instrument so that he could play the tune. Lars the Luthier was known for the clear, singing tones of his guitars.

Jonas falls back into sleep, having never fully awoken, and dreams of guitars of all shapes and sizes. When he wakes to the alarm at 5:30 AM, drinks chai, and walks to the mountain in the cool dawn with a few sangha members, he has a song in his heart.

He gets up from where he has been sitting on some clumps of prickly grass, and stretches, just as the sun begins to peek from behind the mountain. The others have continued to hike farther up the mountain, and he can see them sitting on boulders a little ways up. He is alone.

The song that has been playing within him somewhere, vibrating in his body, wells up into his vocal cords and Jonas lets it come out. He sings a song to Arunachala, to the rising sun, to the birds that begin to join in. The melody plunges and soars and long vowels open his throat until it is no longer he who is singing the song: the song is singing itself through him.

Jonas stands there facing the mountain while the music pours through him. When the sun shows its entire face above the mountain, the song finishes. Jonas walks back toward the ashram, and each step he takes is a new moment, perfect and whole, and he is entirely at peace. The dawn air is soft and still, punctuated by birdsong.

~

Jonas is around halfway through the two-week retreat now. Most of the time he has a clear mind and walks around in a fully present, blissful state, carrying D's words in his heart. But recently other stuff has been happening, like the automatic writing—which makes him wonder about it, which puts him in his head and out of the present, out of bliss and into a kind of curiosity. He hesitates to tell D about the words that have been falling out of his pen, and he wonders about that, too.

And sometimes in the middle of the night he's been waking up with anger ripping through his chest over Carla and Seb and the college where he used to teach. It hurts physically: his chest gets tight and there's a burning feeling right in the center of it. And he lies there as words and scenes replay, torturously, one after the other: first Carla, then Seb, then the chair of the English department. Jonas has learned from D to let it all play out while letting the emotions move through him. Until he can watch it all and feel calm, feel like it doesn't matter. Feel into it until it disappears. Like imagining falling down a well. Until he feels no fear. So he lies there watching it all until his chest relaxes, opens, and he can breathe fully again.

Sometimes he feels that all of this stuff just doesn't matter; it's just stuff coming up, and that's normal in a retreat like this one. But other times he has questions about it. And those questions lead to other questions. Like whether D can really see him. Does he know who Jonas is? He seems to treat Jonas more coolly, more distantly than the others. Jonas wants D to know him like how he seems to know the others here, with that kind of intimacy. And with that love. If he doesn't know me, how can he love me?

Jonas is reminded of the rock opera *Jesus Christ Superstar* and Judas, in his emotional agony, asking if Jesus loves him as he's running to the top of a desert hill to hang himself from a tree. In fact, he thinks about *Jesus Christ Superstar* a lot here—most of his biblical knowledge comes from the Lloyd Webber and Rice musical, which his atheist father introduced to him as a response to young

Jonas's questions about Christianity—and he often finds himself humming one or another of the songs that he knew and loved as a kid. The song Mary Magdalene sings, "I Don't Know How to Love Him," has taken on new meaning, and now Jonas truly understands what she is feeling. He too has been changed and doesn't know what to do.

Is all this stuff just his mind spinning, and should he just let it go? Is it just that he's in the process of "burning away" old issues that come out of his conditioning, as D would say? Burning away the egoic shell that has been built like armor to protect him from pain but that also keeps him away from his true Self? And the burning, if fully experienced, will lead him closer to the Self, to enlightenment, to reality, by thinning the armor, wearing it away? Why does he care so much if D loves him, anyway? Does he smell something burning here?

He has seen others here in great turmoil, exposing their vulnerability and pain, and burning away their egoic shells in cathartic-looking moments with D. Clarissa's body jerks involuntarily, and she told D in satsang that she has been in an extremely uncomfortable state of feeling that she's trying to crawl out of her own skin. And George had been shaking and crying during meditation. One by one they take the chair beside D, and reach a calm there with him, often after breaking down completely.

Jonas admires their bravery. He was brave once, too, right at the start of the retreat, when he cried in D's arms. He felt like a child then. A child in his father's arms. Or maybe it wasn't bravery, but simply following his heart. For a while, anyway, he had no need for any kind of bravery because he had no needs at all. For days his mind was still, and he felt carried by a warm swell of air, filled with a gentle calm. Grace. Beauty. Perhaps these strange writings are another kind of grace, like his name etched on the mountainside. Perhaps even the nighttime torture was a kind of grace. That's what D would tell him, he feels quite sure. And that it all comes up as it should, for him to meet whatever he needs to. Tailor-made just for him. Divinely orchestrated to bring him closer to the Self.

Maybe D would ask, What do the writings mean to him?

That's the thing: he doesn't have a clue.

Now Jonas is noticing moments of, well, irritation. He also feels quite separate from D, and that pains him greatly. It feels like he is being ignored. He barely acknowledges Jonas, in satsang or out. So many people here have close relationships with D. Although they mostly maintain silence outside of satsang, he sees their intimacy in shared looks and hugs and laughter. And in satsang, D often refers to an event or an important person in someone's past, or tells them how far they've come since such-and-such a time. But D doesn't know about Jonas's past, so how could he know how far he's come? Or he mentions how "open" someone is now. Isn't Jonas open? He feels wide open. He feels so much.

And Jonas has seen the odd person knock on the door of D's cottage, and go in. D had told them all at the start that if something came up that was giving them difficulty, and they needed to speak with him, they could knock on his door. Or tack a note for him to the notice board and arrange a private meeting. Jonas feels that jealousy again. And he feels left out. Everyone seems to be closer to D than he is. Jonas wants to change that.

So that evening he writes D a note. Really, more like a letter, quite a long letter. He wants D to know him, at least a little bit. So in the letter, he tells D about himself. And before he can think much about it, before he reconsiders, he folds the letter in quarters, writes "D" on a blank side, and tacks it to the notice board. And waits. He knows D reads his notes at the end of each day.

But the next day comes and goes and another begins, and there is no acknowledgment from D. After morning satsang, Jonas goes to his cottage, closes the curtains, sits down on the edge of his bed, and buries his face in his hands. He feels very alone—more than that, lonely. Why didn't he just take the chair in satsang and talk to D? Why is it all suddenly so hard? He feels he gave a large part of himself away in that letter, and got nothing in return. He knows that feeling well. He had been there often in his life. D says that all of your issues are old; there's nothing new. They just get repeated. And each person has only a few issues. It just seems like more because you keep cycling through them, over and over, in different situations with different people playing the same old roles.

Jonas doesn't want to think about it anymore. He's just pissed off. Screw it. He'll skip lunch and afternoon satsang and take a rickshaw into town. He needs a break.

Tiru is just the same as when he'd left for the retreat, which surprises Jonas a little. He goes to the German Bakery restaurant and eats eggs and drinks coffee—neither of which are available in the ashram. So satisfying. Maybe it's the different vegetarian diet in the ashram that is throwing him off kilter. His body has been craving protein. That's it. It is physiological. He is wasting away. So he eats a chocolate croissant, just for good measure. Then he walks down the street and buys a pack of cigarettes and smokes two at the side of the road, one after the other. He hasn't done that in a while. It feels rebellious. It feels good. If he knew where he could get a beer, he would have. Hell, he'd have downed a few.

Jonas wanders the streets and ventures into Ramana's ashram, half-hoping he'll run into Bruce and they could catch up. He doesn't. And he doesn't want to meditate in the hall or do anything spiritual. In fact, he is sick of being here, sick of all of these seeker types in their flowy outfits, Namaste-ing everybody; ticked off at all the beggars and street vendors who want his money. Fuck 'em all. Fuck everything.

He walks away, and keeps on walking out of town, sticking close to the edge of the road, as far from traffic as possible, brusquely waving away rickshaw drivers who stop to ask if he needs a ride. He walks until he leaves the main town; he walks along a street full of temples where orange-robed, long-bearded sadhus sit and smoke on the side of the road; he walks along a street lined with little hole-in-the-wall restaurants, and tiny shops with glassed-in shelves of colorful orange and yellow sweets, and chai stalls where Indian men stand around and chat, holding little steaming cups in their hands. He walks right up to a travel agency called Ramu's Travel, climbs up the stairs, and enters. He doesn't know why. He is just thinking of getting away.

The place is surprisingly crowded with travelers for being so out of the way. One room is the travel agency, and an adjoining room is full of computers and people talking away on Skype. A few Indian-looking people are roaming about, helping customers. Jonas asks one if he could use a computer. He spends an hour on it, catching up on emails, checking Facebook, messaging friends, and he begins to feel a bit better, more like himself. Like how he used to be, anyway. He doesn't feel up to Skyping though. He is sure he looks like shit.

When his time is up, he goes to the front desk to pay, and he hears a woman's voice that sounds familiar, coming from the computer room he'd just walked out of. Jonas looks around, trying to find the voice's owner. There are too many people, all talking on Skype or to each other. He decides just to leave; it can't be anyone he knows, anyhow. As he passes through the door on the way out, he hears her voice again, and gets a weird feeling. Where has he heard that voice before?

When Jonas finally makes it back to the ashram he is tired from his long walk (he gave in and took a rickshaw for the last stretch), but satisfyingly so. His mood has changed for the better. It's dinnertime, so he goes straight to the dining hall and joins the others in a meal of rice and dal and veg curry with yoghurt, and banana for dessert. When he gets up to wash his stainless steel plate, he finds himself standing next to D at the long communal sink. D speaks to him in a soft voice.

"Hi, Jonas. How are you doing?"

Jonas is taken aback. D doesn't usually initiate contact with anyone.

"Um, I'm better now. Thanks! Sorry I missed satsang."

D looks at him so warmly, it feels like there's no one else in the world but the two of them, and Jonas wonders why he was ever upset.

"Would you like to talk?" D asks him gently, kindly.

"Really? Yes. Yes, I think I would."

"Can you come to my cottage after morning satsang tomorrow, Jonas?"

"You mean just, like, knock on your door?"

D smiles. "Just knock on my door!"

"Sure. I'd like that. Thank you, D. See you tomorrow!"

Jonas returns to his cottage with a big smile on his face. Everything is good again.

CHAPTER 14

Anamika noticed Bruce at Ramu's agency. He came there one day when she was working, and just hung around until she had finished her work. They went for a walk together and bought some fruit at a nearby stall along the way.

He asked if she'd been to the Shiva temple in Tiru, a large complex, one of the largest in India, housing many shrines and halls and statues, and surrounded by four extremely tall gateway towers, covered in intricate carvings. The temple is associated with fire, of course, being dedicated to Shiva who appeared at the top of Arunachala as a flame and is now incarnated in the mountain itself. Fire is one of Hinduism's five elements, which, along with earth, water, and air, includes ether—the subtlest of the elements and the one that underlies and connects them all. The universal element, the space between atoms, the empty void, the spirit. Each element corresponds to the five senses, and the subtler each element is, the fewer the senses needed to perceive it.

The basest element, earth, can be perceived by all five senses: it can be heard, felt, seen, tasted, and smelled. Water, the next subtler element, cannot be smelled; and fire can be heard, felt, and seen, but not smelled or tasted. Air can only be heard and felt. Ether, the most subtle, can't be felt, but it is the medium of sound or vibration. Sound is its only characteristic. Thus ether corresponds to sound.

Aum is the sound of the universe, the creative force in everything and the sound of all sounds heard together. *Aaauuummmm.*

Anamika listened to Bruce describe these fundamental Hindu concepts, and understood that he was telling her about them in order to understand them more fully himself. Or else to show her that he knew things too. She likes Bruce. He has an easiness about him, an openness. She also likes that he is from Vancouver too. And she also likes how he looks. He reminds her of a Greek god, maybe Apollo, the sun god. Tall, blond, and beautiful, with a dazzling smile, and almost too muscular. And he inhabits his body easily, comfortably, not at all self-consciously. He has an innocence and spontaneity. Anamika feels the stirrings of sexual attraction. It has been a long time. What are the rules here? Could a guru mess around with a student?

They make a date to go to the Shiva temple the following day. It's a little ways away, so they plan on taking Anamika's scooter.

As they stroll, they eat the fruit they bought and talk about where they lived and hung out in Vancouver, and juice from the orange Anamika is eating dribbles down her chin. Bruce wipes it away with his finger, and then abruptly excuses himself, as if he'd made a mistake. How sweet, Anamika thinks, and tells him so. He is trying to be so respectful.

The next morning, Bruce gets on the back of Anamika's scooter and they drive to the Shiva temple. It's a tight fit: he's a big guy. Anamika enjoys the feeling of his hard chest against her back and the pressure of his muscular thighs around her legs as she drives. It is such a hot and humid day that when they get off the scooter, they have to peel themselves apart.

Later that day on Anamika's bed, when they peel their sweaty bodies apart from each other, they hear little popping sounds of suction being broken. Pop, pop, pop.

CHAPTER 15

Jonas is nervous and excited. He knocks on the door of D's cottage, and hears a welcoming "Come in!" He removes his flip-flops and enters. And there's D, leading him to a meeting room, a small room obviously separate from his living space. Jonas is a bit disappointed; he was looking forward to seeing D's personal space, his personal things—if he had any, that is.

"Please take a seat."

Jonas chooses a plastic chair, and D pulls another one up and sits close to Jonas.

"Hi, D."

"Hi." D's simple greeting fills Jonas with warmth, and he is immediately at ease.

They sit silently for a few moments. Jonas has left his mind behind and all the questions spinning there. He is fully present with D. Just sitting and looking into his eyes. He notices how light D's eyes are, especially up close like this. Or maybe they are filled with light. He notices that D's pupils are contracted into tiny black points. And the light surrounds it. For such a dark man—olive skin, once-dark hair—he has unusually light eyes.

"Well," says D.

"Well," Jonas responds. And they both laugh.

"Is there something you'd like to talk about?"

"Um, there used to be, like, yesterday. Something that seemed important. But, well, right this moment, I don't know. My thoughts appear to have evaporated!"

D laughs. "I wouldn't want to make you think, just for me!"

A wavering ribbon of light appears in Jonas's mind, and he grasps at the thought before it disappears. "How to put this. I've been feeling, um, left out actually, or ignored. Especially when you didn't respond at all to my letter. But now I think it's kind of funny that I even wrote you a letter about myself in the first place!"

"Thank you for your letter, Jonas. You know, the particulars of a person don't matter to me. That's why I didn't respond. There was nothing for me to say. I don't think, if I remember correctly, that there was a question for me to answer in your letter. If there was, I would have addressed it in satsang."

"I see," Jonas replies. But he isn't satisfied. "I guess I feel that you know most of the people here quite well, and I wanted you to know me, too."

"Yes," D nods as if he understands completely. "I know them because we all live in the same community. But we don't socialize together. I don't socialize. Most of the particulars I know about them, I only know through our many satsangs together. And, again, the particulars aren't important. I feel your essence, your heart, as much as I feel theirs."

Jonas feels a bit better. D seemed to know what he needed.

"Jonas," D looks serious and leans in toward him. "What do you feel left out *of*?"

D holds him with his eyes, and Jonas is overcome with emotion. He dives into a deep dark well and is caught in a vortex, spinning further and further down into blackness.

He feels the pain of his father's lack of attention to him—his ignoring Jonas's great need for his affection. His father's work and girlfriends were always more important than Jonas, more deserving of his precious time. He feels the pain of the English department's decision that his qualifications weren't enough for him to be hired as a regular member of the department. They excluded him from the inner circle and steady employment, after he had given so many years to them, and worked so hard and so well, going above and beyond. He feels the pain of his former best friend's and wife's betrayal when Sebastian told him they'd fallen in love and wanted to be together. Jonas had confided so much in him about his and Carla's faltering marriage, having no idea that Seb himself was playing a part in it. Jonas feels that he's been left out of everything important all of his life.

"D, I can't. I can't…" Jonas breaks down in great loud sobs that rack his body in the plastic chair.

"You don't have to do or say anything. Just feel it. Feel into it. Let the story go." D speaks lovingly, and takes Jonas's hand.

To his surprise, Jonas feels humiliation, as if the worst part of his exclusion is how he thinks other people will perceive him. As not good enough. Unworthy. Foolish even. Unlovable. Nobody really knows him. And if they don't know me, how can they love me?

An image of Jonas's father rises up in him: but here he is looking tenderly at Jonas and tucking him into bed. Jonas burrows under the soft comforter, and sighs sleepily. He feels safe. Cared for. Loved.

Another image quickly follows: his father is sitting across the kitchen table, asking Jonas how his play-date went over half-eaten peanut butter-and-jam sandwiches. Jonas is swinging his legs from the chair as he chatters about his day. He feels happy. Listened to. Seen.

An image of Carla arises: she is doing dishes at the kitchen sink with her back turned toward him, quietly asking Jonas if he doesn't want to know what her day was like.

Another image: the hurt look on her face when Jonas finally peers up from marking student essays to see Carla standing there, patiently waiting for him to see her in her new yellow dress, just before she abruptly turns and leaves the room, slamming the door.

Jonas hears that slam for the first time, it seems. It ricochets in his head. He grows quiet. He sits up, raises his face to D's, and lets go of his hand.

D nods. "Yes, yes. The issue itself is the answer; it is the doorway. Good. Very good."

Jonas gazes out the window. Something has shifted inside of him. Stilled. He looks back at D. And right into his eyes, which go in forever, and which now seem to be wet with tears. And Jonas is flooded with love for him, such tender love, and all at once he understands something, understands it in every love-filled pore of him: all D wants from Jonas, from all of them, is for them to join him. Join him in God, in oneness, in the place where he lives. And for Jonas to give him that, that one thing, he has to cease being himself. That's all.

D closes his eyes, and Jonas senses an energy wafting from D's body—as if he were doing something strenuous but without moving. Jonas closes his eyes, too. And straightens his spine in the chair. Several minutes pass where Jonas feels his whole body tingling with little electric shocks, not unpleasantly. The skin on his calves crawls.

He feels his love for D open into something else. And he goes through that door.

Then comes a sound. A loud sound, right in the top of his head. Like a click. Or a crack. Or a pop. Jonas opens his eyes, startled.

And an ocean sweeps in through the top of his head and out, and Jonas isn't a body at all but part of this ocean, this bliss that is better than any drug. And D and the room and the chairs are part of the ocean that is inside Jonas and that Jonas is inside of at the same time. He isn't separate from anything because there is no "he." There is just this ocean.

D opens his eyes and smiles at Jonas. And Jonas doesn't know who smiled, and it doesn't matter. He and D are the same.

Jonas feels his own voice coming, hears it, but otherwise does not identify with it. It is just a voice saying, "Thank you." And that voice is the ocean too, and it is all love and gratitude.

Jonas leaves D's cottage, returns to his own, sits on his bed in a half-lotus, and closes his eyes.

~

Jonas misses lunch, but attends afternoon satsang and dinner. He is still in the ocean and the ocean is in him; he is everything and everybody. His body sits at satsang and walks to the dining hall, but when he has to do more subtle things with it—like get his stainless steel plate and line up for dinner, turn the plate in his hands as the serving people scoop rice and vegetables on it—it's as if consciousness is being squeezed through a narrow funnel, contracting to the task at hand, and there is a kind of difficulty or pressure there. He moves slowly. When he eats, he is aware of the food being put in the mouth, traveling down the throat and into the digestive system.

Eating is miraculous. Moving the body is miraculous. The spacious dining hall, the warm night air, the assortment of people, all appear within him, as part of him, of God, of the ocean, and it is all beautiful and joyful. Each person and thing is distinct and almost unbearably unique, yet made of the same ineffable, luminous oneness.

When he walks back to his cottage from the dining hall, a peacock accompanies him. At the door of his cottage it fans open its blue-green iridescent eye-feathers, turns around, and struts away. Jonas undresses, lies down on his bed under his sheet, and falls asleep.

When he wakes to his travel alarm at 5:30 AM, he is Jonas again, a separate being, the subject in a dream world of objects. He feels his thoughts move sluggishly in his mind, feels his body, *his* body, *his* mind. The room in his cottage looks like a stage set in a theater: the clothes hanging from the hooks in the wall, the pack of Marlboros sitting on the shelf, the empty red backpack slouching in the corner, even the droppings of gecko shit here and there—all are arranged, in that precise way, for a purpose in the play, to set a scene.

But the taste of the ocean lingers, the sound of its *Aaauuummmm* fills his ears, and Jonas is now standing on its shore, having crawled out from its wet embrace like a prehistoric amphibian taking its first steps on land. He marvels at the light bouncing crystals off the waves and the wet spray of shimmering rainbows in the air as the waves rush in to shore. And he longs to be immersed in that again.

CHAPTER 16

Bruce comes to Anamika's place before satsang with eggs and onion and chapati, and makes them both onion omelets for breakfast. After eating, while they are drinking chai, he plugs his iPod in and plays a sitar-tabla piece for her. The strains of the sitar move through the air, opening long spaces in it, and then the tabla drumbeats come, perforating the spaces, *tikka-tikka dhaaaa, tikka-tikka dhaaa*, and Anamika and Bruce dance. The room opens with sound, and spaces in the air open into other spaces, and everything everywhere is dancing in and out of the spaces. Light flickers and swirls.

When the music ends, Anamika glances at the clock. 11:11. Hi, Mom. That was nice, wasn't it? And now there is a different kind of sound, coming from outside her door—gentle knocks, murmuring. Anamika lets the people in and begins satsang.

"Today, we'll begin with a different kind of meditation. Does everyone have room to stand up and move around a bit? Good. Imagine you are standing waist-deep in a warm ocean. Move your arms slightly away from your body, and back and forth, letting your fingers run through the water around you. Feel the softness of the water, the tingles at the ends of your fingers. Nice.

"Now let your arms move any way they want to."

The people gathered sway their bodies with the motion of their arms. Some begin to move their feet a little.

"Now let your whole body move any way it wants. Let your feet move, your hips, your torso, shoulders, head. Feel the dance move through you."

The room begins to fill with movement, choppy and hesitant at first. Sita doesn't move at all until she looks at Gabi who is lifting her knees up and down a little, one at a time. She shyly imitates Gabi's knee-lifts and begins to move like Gabi. Gabi smiles warmly at her and nods her head. Sita nods her head. Sita then twists her torso to the left and right, while still lifting her knees and moving her arms in ever-widening sweeps. Gabi follows Sita's movement. Sita laughs. She feels like she's never felt before—like a bhangra dancer in a Bollywood movie! She is leading a dance. Gabi is following her. For the first time in her adult life, Sita feels seen and acknowledged by another person.

A few more people take on the moves of the people around them. There are happy smiles and laughter at this trading of movement, of acknowledging through imitation each other's ways of moving their bodies. One moves this way, and another moves this way. The other moves that way, and another moves that way. And back and forth, movements are exchanged and shared, until there arises a natural fluidity among all the dancers. They are sharing the very same dance, dancing as one body with many limbs.

"Is there a sound in your body? Let it come out. You are composed of sound, and your vibrating cells sing to each other. Your fluid body is singing like a river. Let the song of your body come out."

Different sounds move through the air in waves: long, low sonorous tones; high, ringing, bell-like tones; rhythmic drum-like staccato sounds. The dance changes with the vocalizations; they are now riding the waves, dancing on the waves of sound.

Anamika joins in the song and dance. She isn't aware of time passing, but at one point, she hears the voices in the room becoming one sound, full and rich and multi-tonal—and sees the people dancing together in their colorful loose clothing as trees, forests, rivers, oceans. They are one body with many arms, Shiva, dancing the world into being. And the world is the room, the room is the world, and the sound soaring from their one joined voice is *Aaauuummmm*.

The sound crests and begins its gradual descent to silence; the dance slows as the sound falls. Soon, everyone is only slightly swaying and moving their arms gently around their bodies. Anamika can see tiny white sparks of electricity flying from their fingers and jumping high between their swaying bodies, emitting little sounds.

The song-and-dance meditation has caused a stir among the people at Anamika's satsang. Afterward, there are exclamations of "Wow!" and "That was amazing." It's obvious that people want to share their experiences with each other. So Anamika suggests a ten-minute break for chatting and going outside to breathe the air and let their sweat dry off.

Once the group gathers again in Anamika's room (which is feeling a little like a sauna now), Sita's hand rises. She speaks with a strength and volume that Anamika has not heard before in her. "Anamikaji, we have been talking with each other, and several of us are wondering if you would be so kind as to be telling us what you are knowing about matters regarding the body, such as health and illness, these things."

"Sitaji, I would be most pleased to do this. Thank you for asking."

The group waits expectantly, faces glistening with perspiration. Anamika closes her eyes as she searches for a way into this dense forest of a subject. When she opens her eyes, the words fall out slowly and easily, one after the other.

"Your body is your own. It is, simply, you. It is not something 'alien,' as Ramana is reported to have once said, neither is it a temple in which your soul is housed. Each cell is yours, and reflects who you are as surely as the clothes you chose to wear today, how you style your hair, as surely as the shape of your face and body, the lines on your palm. And as surely as the world around you, the reality that you project from your deeply held assumptions and beliefs, which is yours uniquely. You make your body in the same way. It does not exist separately from you.

"When your body is not healthy, it doesn't mean that something is 'wrong' and needs to be fixed—whether you believe it was you who ultimately caused the health problem (by smoking or getting run-down or whatever) or it just occurred. It is not that 'health is positive' and 'illness is negative.' In fact, like all dualities, the conceptual categories of 'positive' and 'negative' are over-simplifications and ultimately meaningless. And anyway, 'positive' exists only through its opposite, 'negative,' so when you tell yourself to 'be positive' you're really saying 'don't be negative'—which, by virtue of the word 'don't,' is literally, grammatically, negative! And there you are, caught up in a fight with yourself. And that certainly doesn't promote health, wholeness. 'Positive thinking' might be popular in the wellness industry, but championing one side of anything polarizes the field into opposing teams that are good and bad and who win and lose. Really, like the yin-yang symbol, each duality contains within it the seed of the other, its 'opposite.' And if you spin this circular yin-yang symbol like a wheel, you'll see that its two separate paisley halves blur together and become one.

"The make-up of your body is constantly in flux, ever-changing, like your environment, and like sub-atomic particle-waves. It is subtly and faithfully transforming the beliefs you hold about yourself and the world into chemicals, hormones, cellular and electrical movements and patterns. There is a deeply personal interchange between your continuously dying-rebirthing cells and your evolving self. The astoundingly complex and delicate forces that make up your solid-appearing physical form don't just tick along by themselves, fed by whatever other physical things you give it, like food, air, water, medicine, acupuncture, yoga postures, exercise, whatever. They react and respond to your perceptions and interpretations of what's around you.

"The effect of stress and trauma is one small example among many of how this works. Western medicine now knows beyond a doubt that trauma has a direct physiological effect, and therapies for trauma now involve the body. The 'fight-or-flight response' is a biological mechanism that kicks in when a threat is *perceived*, and post-traumatic stress disorder, or PTSD, originates in a person's inability to either fight or flee the perceived threat at the time. The nervous system freezes, and the energy gets stuck there. Unresolved trauma creates a multitude of physiological and psychological symptoms and illnesses; PTSD is long-term and debilitating and sometimes fatal. And what is a threat to one person is not necessarily to another. It depends on you. It's personal, subject to interpretation.

"Neuroscience has taken the interdependent relationship between thought and body even further: it tells us that we change the very structure of our brains by what we think and do. And even imagine! And dream. Imagine that: our dreams change the physicality of our brains. And many people think 'my brain is who I am; it makes me, me.' Nope, it is only another reflected manifestation of who you really are beyond your physical self. We literally *imagine* ourselves. And anyhow, if 'my brain is me,' then neuroscience is revealing that who we are comes from our imagination, our thoughts, which in turn come from what we believe at a fundamental level. What we call a brain is barely a physical entity anyway ('mind' and 'brain' are constantly conflated) but rather an intricate, ever-changing, malleable network of buzzing electrical activity. Neural pathways are carved out and deepen the more they are traveled, and thus certain beliefs, perspectives, even memories, are reinforced as solid, rigid 'facts' about the world or oneself. But new pathways are constantly being created, and even the well-traveled ones can change and disappear—and with them, the kind of world that they previously affirmed as real.

"Like your life, your body is an intimate expression of who you are, a living art form that you are constantly creating. If the body had a more solid, objective reality—were truly just a bundle of bones and sinew—it wouldn't be such a scientific mystery, so difficult to treat medically and subject to endless permutations of healing modalities and ideas about wellness. Like traditional indigenous healers, the best western doctors know that medicine is an art, not a science. There's always an element of creative intuition—if not magic—in a cure.

"Again, let me emphasize, illness doesn't mean that you are out of balance, wrong, not in harmony somehow, as some kinds of wellness practitioners might have us believe. (Did you forget to align your chakras today? Have you been wallowing in negative thoughts?) Your illness isn't your 'fault.' It only means that you have something to do that's very special and of particular importance to you. The sick person is in the process of self-discovery and ultimately self-transformation—which, as we know, is never easy. In fact, it is the most difficult thing one can do. You are literally risking your life. And you don't risk your life for just anything.

"The supposed physical 'cause' of your illness doesn't matter. What does matter is what it means to you. What part or system of your body is experiencing the problem? How do you see this body part or system? In your own personal mythology, what does it symbolize? Interpret the metaphor of your illness. Once you do that, and if the interpretation feels right to you, there will be a shift, a transformation. Only when our wounds are revealed can they be healed.

"When you are ill, the illness is what you need right now. You have brought it into your life for an intimate, important purpose. Even if there is great pain and suffering. Here is something for you to explore, to engage with, to learn from. *Your illness is calling your attention to something.* Sometimes it is simply reminding you to turn your focus inward, to honor a life transition by slowing down. Sometimes it is asking you to do something more difficult: to shift perspectives about something. Other times it is asking nothing less than an overhaul of your entire belief system: it is asking you to change your perceptions about yourself and the world, to create new interpretations, new neural pathways, a new life. Often it is doing all of these. As I'm sure you know, it's not uncommon for those who have recovered from a lengthy, serious illness to be grateful for it, for what it taught them.

"One is never doing battle with an outside force bent on destruction, as a common 'well vs. sick' analogy goes. There's that 'positive and negative' ruse again. You supposedly either win the battle with courage and resilience, or you lose it, after putting up a 'brave fight.' (The Big C is a common conqueror in this scenario.) The existence of highly contagious viruses heightens this perspective: they're out there and will get you if you're not careful! Your body must therefore be separate from *you* and vulnerable to attack. War metaphors abound.

"This analogy is built on the belief that you can be attacked from an outside force—or it may be an inside-body job, depending on the illness, an unfortunate genetic condition, which really has nothing to do with you. Bad luck! Or suddenly the cells that make up your body become the enemy as they start multiplying, differentiating, and then you're at war with cancer.

"Nothing could be further from the truth. You are fighting your very own cells. You are only fighting yourself. Look inside yourself; look inside your body.

"Sickness is always an internal journey because it forces you into yourself, to concentrate on healing, to bringing forth what needs to be looked at. This is true whether it's a cold, a stubbed toe, a car accident injury, a contagious virus, or cancer. They all make you slow down and turn your attention away from the busy outside world, for just a moment or for years. Of course, you can take vitamin C for a cold, breathe through the passing pain of a stubbed toe, get a cast for a broken leg, vaccine for the virus, chemo for cancer, and you may very well get better. These treatments are one culture's ways to heal, and you have invested energy and belief in these cures, in these visions. The physical is a manifestation, whether it's the sickness itself or the means of addressing it.

"Medical treatments are often successful because they allow the patient to surrender to something perceived as outside of themselves and to thus help them release their fear, to feel looked after, in good, expert hands. In any case, because fear has a constricting effect (you know what it does to just your breathing!) it's beneficial to release fear about your illness, and that means finding a way to keep in the present moment, to not worry about a future, to not give the mind permission to paint scenarios. Instead, paint a picture with a paintbrush, with your fingers, engage your senses, your body. You can also heal by chanting *Aum* and breathing fully, or doing whatever kind of activity feels good to you: like gentle yoga or stretching or singing or dancing, taking a bath, giving yourself a little massage—and resting, letting your body do its own work. I like singing and chanting in the shower, myself! There's a kind of alchemy that occurs when sound vibrations and water meet skin—a deep, organic penetration, perhaps a cellular recollection of being in the watery womb, feeling sounds in the mother's life-sustaining body. But that's just me. Find your own way to open your body to its own innate vitality.

"Your body's 'normal' state is health, wholeness. On one level, the body is already whole, at ease. The 'dis-ease' exists because there is something you need to do now, for yourself, for your ever-widening capacity to grow, learn, and rediscover who you are.

"Sickness is an opportunity. Take it."

~

"Here is an exercise that will help promote wellness. Let's all do this right now, even though we may be feeling good at the moment. You can remember it for the times that you'll need it. Get yourselves in a comfortable position."

There is a shifting about on the floor and moving around of the cushions that some people have brought with them.

"Okay? Nice and comfy? Now, turn your focus on wherever you feel discomfort—your chest, sinuses, leg, hip, guts, head. Go inside of it. Experience the feelings there as fully as you can. Sink into the feelings. Deeply. As deeply as you can. And let's just stay there for a while.

"Let whatever images that are there come forth. Watch the image, let it evolve. What does it look like? What color is it? What is its shape? Does it have a texture? If words come out of the feeling in your uncomfortable area, say the words; if there are sounds, make the sounds. If you want to make a movement, a gesture, do so. Let your body speak to you in whatever way it wants. Listen and watch carefully for its messages, then express them yourself in whatever way feels right. Do this for a few minutes, then stop."

Some people make small movements; some make sounds and words. Kris stands up and does a forward bend. Anamika wishes she had some crayons for creating colorful visual images.

"Breathe fully; feel the breath throughout your entire body. Concentrate on your full breath for a few minutes.

"Then go back into the discomfort and find what's there again. See if it has changed. Alter the expression you made before to reflect this new state. Do this for a while, then stop. There is a world inside your body. Be an explorer! Take the risks you need in order to find what you're looking for.

"If you are sick, and you spend a bit of time each day on this, listening to your body and what it has to tell you—heeding its messages—there *will* be changes, and you will feel better. You will begin to recover, if that is what you, ultimately, want to do.

"Your body is your own, an intimate reflection of yourself. Your body is the best teacher there is for you. Why? Because it *is* you. You are you.

"The resolution to the problem is in the problem itself. The medicine is in the illness."

CHAPTER 17

The day after Jonas's swim in the ocean, there is friction during satsang. Something strange is going on, tempers are flaring. There is a dispute between two sangha members during breakfast, and one of them storms out of the dining hall. Jonas sees the other one talking quietly to D. And that's another thing: more and more people are talking to each other, sometimes laughing together in little groups. Jonas, who is keeping silent, starts to feel left out again.

Are things changing because the halfway mark of the retreat has passed and the home stretch lies ahead? Are people getting anxious about the future, about heading home and getting back to "real life"? Before the friction of today, everyone in the ashram behaved lovingly and kindly toward each other. It was like living in a kind of utopia. Where everyone hugged a lot.

But was this love, though many-splendored, temporary? Yesterday Jonas had known it as eternal, timeless, and everywhere. Was that a different kind of love? Is true love with a capital "L" the only real kind, and what we know in the world are just poor facsimiles of it? Yet that's the love that people most often die and kill for—romantic love, familial love, the love that lives in the world of longing and fear.

Uh-oh, Jonas thinks. I'm back in my head again. Back in the dream world, which Jonas now thinks of as contained within a bubble. He brushes up against the bubble-world's rubbery edges, and feels them give a little. He wants to pop it again, pierce through that transparent membrane and be in that ultimate reality, where there are no painful divisions between anything and anybody, no friction, no desires or fears or jealousies or regrets, no rigorous mental gymnastics. No edges. Where he is carried, lifted, and dissolved. Where he doesn't have to do anything at all. But just be.

Jonas has no idea what's next for him, after the retreat, and it doesn't seem to matter much. His life is open-ended. He wants to experience being here at the ashram with D, at the foot of this magic mountain, in strange and wondrous India, as fully as he can. So he tries to let thoughts of the future be in the future. And empties his mind of thoughts and questions about real life and fake life, real love and fake love, as well as he can.

At morning satsang, Dauriya has an unusual outburst. Usually very quiet and sweet, she tears into D.

"What are you telling us this time? You say one thing, then another that contradicts it. How can I believe anything you say? You aren't a good teacher. You are confusing!"

"Dauriya, sweetie, I'm not telling you anything."

"See?" Dauriya looks around at the others gathered in the meditation hall. "What does that even mean? Of course you are! You make no sense." She bursts into angry tears and gets up and leaves the hall.

There is a hush. Dauriya's friend follows her.

Everyone is silent for a time. Then D speaks.

"I probably do contradict myself," he says. And laughs. A few people laugh with him. "But, you know, it's not about the content of the words. It's what they do. The words are the pointing. Listen with your heart, not your mind. If you listen just to *what* I say, you should probably get up and leave right now. You'd be better off reading a book on the subject."

The silence deepens. Jonas doesn't know if he should feel chastised or not. Did D just call them out? He looks around. A few people shift on their cushions, but most are sitting peacefully with their eyes closed.

"What you see here, as D, is a reflection of yourself. I will bring up for you what you need to see about yourself right now. I am whoever you want me to be. And through this meeting with yourself, you will burn away whatever your conditioning has thrown up as an obstacle in your path. That is the work. And when the work is done, I won't exist anymore. I will disappear because I am no longer necessary to you."

The meditation hall grows peaceful again. D looks at all gathered there with such love on his face that Jonas feels an ache in his heart.

"You are here because you are ready. If you weren't, you wouldn't be here. It is time for you to do the work. For some of you, the path may be long. You have obstacles in your path that need to be burned away. Your karmic load is heavy. Others have a lighter load. And there are a rare few, like some of the great masters, who enter this life without any karma at all.

"But anyone, the burdened and unburdened, can wake up in an instant." D snaps his fingers.

"I am only your doorway. Walk through me and become who you really are. Walk through me to your freedom."

D smiles. "I probably contradicted myself at least once there."

One thing about silence that Jonas does not like is there is no music. Jonas misses it. Back home, he played a bit of guitar and even wrote a few songs. He knows that the silence code is here to keep people focused and away from the habitual distractions of talking and creating relationships and the self-identification that emerges from that. And to help quiet the chit-chat in one's mind. Or reveal it. To break the hypnotic trance that we are in. But music can be meditative, even devotional—appropriate here. It can take you out of your head and put you into your heart. When Jonas is lost in a piece of music, whether he's hearing it or playing it himself, he leaves himself and his mind behind, and is completely in the moment. Music is like meditation that way.

Jonas recalls the nighttime writing about Lars the Luthier, and how he sang to Arunachala the next morning at dawn. He is now longing for music, to be surrounded by it, immersed in it. He doesn't think he's experienced anything he could describe as "longing" in his Vancouver life—with the possible exception of when he first saw Carla—and now it keeps coming up, opening him up. It occurs to him that this longing may be directly related to yesterday's immersion in the ocean of love, and is part of that longing to be in it again. Maybe now every desire he feels will be directly related to that. Ultimately speaking, that is.

Jonas remembers that when he was staying at Mountain View Towers in Tiruvannamalai, every evening at 7:30 PM at Ramana's ashram there was a kirtan, the playing and singing of devotional songs or bhajans. He and Bruce attended one, and it was amazing. Three Indian musicians expertly played harmonium, tabla, and a stringed instrument Jonas hadn't seen before, on a little stage in the main hall, and led the hundreds of mainly Indians gathered there, and some foreigners, in singing and chanting. The sound and feeling of so many voices melodically dipping and soaring in Sanskrit was uplifting and deeply satisfying. Jonas wants that again.

So after dinner he takes a rickshaw to Ramana's ashram in Tiru. He wonders if he'll see Bruce there.

Jonas finds a place to squeeze in and sits cross-legged on the white marble floor amidst the Indian men (women are on the other side of the hall, segregated for "modesty" purposes). And he gets lost, deliciously, in the heart-full rising of voices, the percussive pulse of the tabla, the full, lingering chords of the harmonium, the strains of the strings. The sound surrounds him, and he is carried, lifted, and dissolves in it.

Afterward, feeling happily satiated, he finds his way to the residential section of the ashram and inquires after Bruce. He wants to leave him a note telling him when the retreat is over so they can arrange a chai together.

The man double-checks the registry with the names of guests handwritten in it. Bruce's name isn't there. He must have left. Was he still in Tiru? Jonas thinks Bruce would have left word at D's retreat if he were leaving town. Still, why would he leave Ramana's ashram if he were still here somewhere? Since neither of them have cell phones (or "mobiles," as they're called here), they have no way of contacting each other. Jonas wonders if they'll ever see each other again.

CHAPTER 18

Anamika can't just do her work like before at Ramu's travel agency because she is often interrupted by people who come to see her especially and ask about when her next satsang will be. She doesn't have a fixed schedule but makes it up as she goes along, leaving time to get her two days a week of work in. Ramu doesn't seem to mind; his business continues to flourish, and Anamika seems to be a part of his rise in profile. Anamika hopes that not too many more people will come to her little place for satsang. It's already crowded with the twenty or so that she invites in regularly. And the ones who have been coming usually come back.

The original five attend every satsang. And Bruce has started to hang out at Ramu's agency when Anamika is working. Sometimes he helps her do her errands and answer customer questions about using the internet. Ramu likes Bruce, and they often talk together when there's a lag in business. When he comes by, he always brings chai and snacks for Ramu and Anamika.

She doesn't know what, if anything, is going on with her and Bruce. She just enjoys his company. He's light-hearted and open. Easygoing. Gentle. And sex with him is good. Great, even. They've enjoyed each other's bodies twice now. And he's a good cook! Bruce found a room not far from Anamika's place, and the evening after the last satsang, he invited her over for dinner. He whipped up something spicy with eggs, mushrooms, and some other vegetable she hadn't seen before, and served it over rice—all cooked up in a pot and a pan on his little hot plate. It was a nice change from Anamika's more simple meals.

At Anamika's next satsang, there is a young woman with Sita who shares her facial features and slim build, only she wears a snug pink-and-orange salwar kameez instead of a faded yellow sari. She introduces herself as Priya, Sita's daughter. Her English is a little clumsy, but good.

"My mother is changing since she is seeing you. She has told me about you and some of the things you are telling her. Then, I am worried about who she is mixing with. We are a traditional Hindu family. We go to temple. Now, my mother is becoming more happy. She dances for my father and giggles like a girl. She sings when we are making food for the family. I am here to thank you for making pleasure in my mother."

It has obviously taken Priya some effort to make this speech, but now she gives Anamika a stunning white-teeth smile, and puts her palms together. Her bangles tinkle on her wrists.

"I'm very happy to hear this, Priya. Thanks for coming by! Will you stay?"

"If it is no problem."

"Of course not. You're very welcome here."

Sita has been smiling shyly during their conversation, and now she falls on her knees and touches Anamika's feet. Anamika knows this is a way of showing respect, and a great honor to bestow upon a younger person, but she feels somewhat embarrassed.

"Thank you, Sita," she says as Sita rises, and she and Priya find a place to sit on Anamika's floor. More people arrive and sit down quietly, some on cushions they've brought with them.

Anamika sits quietly in her chair. She takes in everyone there, and closes her eyes. When she opens them, she asks people to open their ears and just listen.

"Listen to the sounds in this room, the sounds from outside in the street, in the sky, the sounds in your body. Let's just listen for a while."

Anamika hears the nasal moo of a cow outside. Male voices calling and laughing. A bird cawing. A gurgle in her tummy. Someone sniffing. A cough. Labored breathing. A vehicle rattling noisily. Insects buzzing. Dishes clattering. A whirring in her ears. Her mother's voice singing.

"Golden slumbers kiss your eyes, smiles awake you when you rise. Hush little Anna don't you cry, and I will sing a lullaby."

Her mother's voice is beautiful and crystal clear, and she sings softly to Anna at her bedside a special song she created just for her, adapted from Thomas Dekker's 17th century poem, "Cradle Song." She sings the lullaby again, and begins to walk out of Anna's bedroom, the song fading as she tiptoes through the door, leaving it a little ajar.

"Lullaby, lullaby, and I will sing a lullaby. Lullaby, bye, bye."

Anamika opens her eyes and there are tears of love in them. Her vision blurs as she gazes out at the men and women gathered in a semi-circle around her, most of them with closed eyes. She is overcome with gratitude for everyone who has put so much trust in her. How can it be that she has been given this honor to be with these people, to share what's in her heart with them, to give them her words? She puts her palms together in Namaste, and closes her eyes again, sinking deep into humility. When she opens them again, everyone in the room has their palms together and is looking at her.

"I want to thank you with all of my heart for joining me here in satsang. I am very grateful for each and every one of you." She speaks quietly, still overcome with emotion.

"You know, it's really all about listening. Everything is. Being compassionate is being a listener. Compassion is love listening. Being aware is being a listener. Awareness is Self listening.

"Listen with your inner senses. Open your listening self until all you are is listening. When someone speaks to you, like I'm doing right now, try listening this way. Don't wait to speak; don't track your reaction; don't provide an internal commentary; don't anticipate what the speaker might say. Don't think of yourself at all. Don't even think. Just listen. Listen with all of you."

Anamika stops talking when she senses the attention in the room shift, become more open, receptive, the clutter of thoughts die down. Many of those gathered here are truly listening. She can hear it.

"Yes. Okay. Lovely. Now, would anyone like to ask a question?"

CHAPTER 19

Jonas is very aware that there are only a couple of days left in the retreat. He feels like a lifetime has passed here. In the pre-dawn, he walks to the rooftop. There is no one there. He sits with his eyes closed, feeling the stillness within him and without, feeling his being, his heart. Feeling the mountain.

He can hear D's words inside of him: "Just this. The stillness, the silence, and the feeling of your own being. Rest in the silence of what is eternally now. The feeling of your heart. This is all. This is everything. Fall into it."

Jonas breathes in and out. His breath breathes him. He surrenders to that.

He feels the mountain breathing in and out. His breath breathes the mountain. The mountain breathes him in. He surrenders to the mountain, O Arunachala. And his heart overflows with gratitude.

A chant-song plays on his lips, a bhajan he heard at the kirtan in Ramana's ashram, and he sings it aloud: "Aruna-chala Shiva, Aruna-chala Shiva, Aruna-chala Shiva, Arunachalaaaa."

Jonas feels his heart opening like a flower, but never-ending.

Before he rises, he shifts from his half-lotus to a kneeling position, and lays his long torso on the floor of the rooftop, in child's pose. A light breeze blows and tousles his long unruly hair, like his father used to. He stands and touches his palms in Namaste to the mountain, and walks back to his cottage.

He lies on his back on the bed, and still feels his heart opening. It's a physical sensation. Delicate pink petals spread apart, one after the other. Now his heart is completely exposed, big and bloody and dark red, wet and soft and vulnerable, almost painful. He remembers a tall statue he saw in town of the monkey warrior-god Hanuman: he was holding the flesh of his own chest open, peeled back, and exposing his big red heart.

Jonas realizes with a start that this is how his father must have looked like on the operating table when he was having open-heart surgery years ago. Jonas had just moved out on his own and was beginning his adult life. He never went to the hospital to visit him.

On his bed in his cottage, Jonas feels a big thump in his heart. There, in the center of his chest, right on his heart chakra, is a gecko! He didn't even notice any geckoes in the room this morning. Did it fall from the ceiling? Do geckoes even do that? He sits up, laughs, and brushes it off. A gecko. Drawn right to his heart. His big, exposed, vulnerable heart.

Something shifts in Jonas, and he feels a visceral pang of joy. Life is incredible. What a dream this is! The breakfast bell rings, and Jonas is suddenly ravenous.

CHAPTER 20

Priya tentatively raises her hand with a question. "Anamikaji, could you please be speaking to us about relationships? Please forgive me if you are speaking on these things before. I am having many-many difficulties with my friend Sudha who is soon to be marrying a boy from my home village. Sudha and I have been very good friends many-many years, but now she is not stopping asking me about this boy and I, and how we are knowing each other in our home village. She seems to be suspecting of myself that I am not telling her the true-true things about the friendship of Raj and myself. But I am. And I am very very sad in the heart that she is suspecting myself of such things." Priya places her hand over her heart.

"Thank you for the question, Priya," Anamika begins. She looks closely into Priya's eyes which have begun to tear up, and speaks gently.

"Do you know what you look like to other people? Do you know what they see when they look at you? I'm not talking about the image you see of yourself in a mirror, but how you are perceived. People are very interested in what other people think of them, how they see them—what they think of how they look, their clothes, their hair, their body, and how others would describe their personality: are they outgoing, shy, smart, generous, rude? Why are we so concerned about this? Because we can never know how other people see us. And it drives us crazy!"

Some people laugh at this. Anamika can hear Bruce's distinct chortle rise above the others.

"Each of us can only see through our own perceptions, yes? I am a different person to you, Priya, than I am to anyone else. You see me through whatever else you have with you in this moment, and through what you've heard about me from your mother, and through the lens of your culture, and through what you keep from other moments you've shared with me. All of this and more creates who I am to you.

"Sure, there are some consistencies in how others see me: I am short and slight, have long dark curly hair and olive skin. I think my nose is too big for my face and my eyes are too small and close together. I'm good with language and performing, I'm pretty intelligent and seem to know a bunch of stuff, and I can carry a tune well. I think I'm thoughtful and kind to others.

"But see how I've added my own perceptions of myself there? Someone else might not think my nose is big or my eyes are small; someone else might not think I'm thoughtful and kind, but maybe full of myself, a cocky know-it-all. Someone else might not think I know anything at all, certainly nothing of any value or truth. Someone else might think I'm delusional and off my meds! The fact that I'm short and have dark hair might not even be as much of a fact to others, either. It depends on who is doing the perceiving, doesn't it.

"Each of us looks out of our own eyes at the world and each other. We can't really see ourselves, even in a mirror. So who are we to others, really? A collection of our characteristics, like the ones I just named for myself? Where is the consistent character that each of us presents to the world—the whole, finally describable, person?

"Here's the thing. That separate person's existence is as changeable and slippery as those sub-atomic bits that are supposedly the basis of all 'solid matter,' that are really both waves *and* particles simultaneously, depending on if they are being perceived or not. In other words, just as matter's independent existence is suspect, so is the independent existence of other people suspect too.

"On a very real level, nobody else exists. It's just you. There's nothing out there.

"Think of it this way: there is only relationship, and only relationship *to you*. Your relationship with your friend is unique; no one else has that same relationship. It is a special dynamic. You perceive your friend a certain way, different from anyone else's perception of her. Is your perception of your friend really your friend? Of course not. Sure, you can describe her, what she looks like, her behavior, and others will recognize who you are talking about—'Oh, that's Sudha, the one who is getting married to Raj.' And you might have created your own history of who you are together, built on moments that you've shared.

"But even when you're in that moment together, you're not really being with her. You might enjoy being with who you think is Sudha, but your enjoyment is because of how you feel when you're with her. Your friend is a reflection of you, and if you like what is being reflected to you, you enjoy her 'company,' what she 'brings out' in you. But she doesn't bring out these same qualities in other people. No one can really see her, just as no one can really see you.

"So, Priya, in an important way, you exist to your friend Sudha as a reflection of herself. She is creating you. And right now, Sudha is having fears about her marriage, and she is seeing you as the cause of those fears. In this way, she is forced to deal with them because they are creating difficulty in a relationship that presumably she's always treasured, the one she has with you. There are only relationships, and those relationships ultimately point you back to yourself, as they reflect your different issues back to you and show you yourself.

"In the same way, Sudha is showing you *your*self, Priya, reflecting yourself back to you. You yourself are creating Sudha, 'your' Sudha. The difficulties you spoke of having with her are showing you something that you want to know about yourself, and you need to do some exploring to find out what it is. You've given yourself this challenge. It's all about you."

As Anamika winds up her talk, she can't read the expression on Priya's face. "I hope I have provided some kind of answer to your question."

"Thank you, Guruji," Priya mutters quietly, with her head down.

~

"Okay, let's do a 'Just me' meditation, and some writing after so we can explore ourselves a bit. Maybe this will help bring it all home. Bruce, will you help me pass out paper and pens please?"

The group, about twenty-five of them now squeezed into her little room, seem restless, so Anamika suggests a ten-minute break to stretch and chat. She's happy to see Priya return with the rest and take her seat beside her mother.

Anamika speaks quietly and rhythmically.

"Please make yourself comfortable. Let's close our eyes. Imagine that it's just you sitting in a room. Just you, alone. There's no one else here. It's just you in a room by yourself. You don't have to think of anyone else. All relationships fall away. Take a deep breath and let it out slowly. You have no thoughts of anybody. Why should you? It's just you. Feel the relief that comes with knowing that. Ahhhh. Breathe deeply through your nose from your belly, up through your lungs, and out through your mouth. What a relief. It's just me.

"There's just me here. Say it to yourself. Like you mean it. Just me. That you know it's just you, there's no one else around: no one to watch you, to make demands on you, to judge you, to compare yourself with—no one to deal with in any way at all. There's just you alone in this room.

"Just me. It's just me. There's no need to think about it. No need to think about anything. I know who I am. I am comfortable with myself. So comfortable. I love myself. It's just me here. No one else. No one else anywhere. What peace. It's just me.

"Feel the relief of knowing it's just me. Whew. It's flooding my body. I am calm and quiet. It's just me. Just me."

Anamika feels the room still, and she stops talking. All is quiet for ten minutes.

"When you feel ready, open your eyes. Pick up the pen in front of you. Write for five minutes about how it feels to know it's just me. Don't stop writing, let your pen move across the paper. Write in any language you are comfortable in. This is just for you. It's just you here. It's all about you."

When five minutes are up, Anamika speaks again.

"Good. Now I'd like you to bring a relationship you have with someone into your consciousness. There is the person you have this relationship with. Envision the person. Notice how that feels in your body. Where in your body is this feeling? Keep breathing.

"Now let's write once more. This time, write for five minutes non-stop about how you see this person. Write from that place in your body. If you don't know how to start, imagine that you are walking down a street and you see the person walking toward you. How does she or he look? What do you feel in your body and what do you think about as you see him coming toward you? Tell a story about him, if you like."

After the exercise ends, Anamika says, "Now you have two pieces of writing about yourself. Even that story about the other person is really about you. Sometime tomorrow, take a look at these two stories and compare them. Read them as being about the same person. And see what you have told yourself in them. If you want to write about what you have discovered, go ahead."

The satsang ends, and Anamika feels like being by herself, but the people linger in her room, talking to each other. Some are reading their writing aloud to each other. Anamika walks out of her place and down the street a ways. No one notices. When she returns to her room, she is happy to see it empty. As she collects the pens and paper, she notices a little pile of different kinds of paper sitting on her shelf. Rupees, in different denominations. And a little orange marigold. A piece of candy. A piece of paper with a drawing of a tree on it and a big "Thank you!" at the bottom. Gifts. Donations.

Anamika is grateful for the offerings. She could use the money, too. But she needs another, bigger, space in which to hold these sessions.

CHAPTER 21

It is the last day of the retreat, and Jonas wakes up with a poem already made, waiting to be written down.

Bright batches of lemons fall
from a cart in the road,
yellow pools at his feet
the smell tart in the air

What have you to offer but this?
You pick one up off the dirt road
wipe it on your sleeve
hold it tentatively out toward him

He laughs with all the love
in the world for you
takes it to his lips, and bites

Reading it brings tears to Jonas's eyes—the small, spontaneous offering from one who has nothing, and the man who has such love that he bites into the hard, sour rind of the lemon joyfully, as if it's the sweetest fruit there is. And the meaninglessness of "sweet" and "sour" to one whose senses are tuned to the taste of eternity. Perhaps to him it is indeed the sweetest fruit.

After breakfast, Jonas walks slowly to the meditation hall for the last satsang. At noon, the silence code will be broken, and the sangha will gather to share songs and stories before they pack up and leave the ashram. Many here are returning together to the States with D, to the community they all share. Others, like Jonas, are going their own way.

Each day of the retreat, some of the sangha members prepare the meditation hall for that day. In the early morning, they sweep away the leaves and twigs that have blown in overnight, as well as the occasional gecko, spider, or frog that has found its way there. One woman arranges flowers in vases that are placed on the dais. Another lights the candle in front of Ramana's framed photo on the table beside D's chair. These preparations bring a palpable peace to the hall, so that when one enters, one can feel the personal care that has gone into creating the space, and sink into the calm.

Jonas takes his seat, breathes deeply, and, as usual, takes a few moments to appreciate the beauty of the dais on which D will take his place after the sangha finishes meditating: the colorful flowers in the vases, the framed photo of the gently smiling Ramana, the reflection of the candle flame flickering in the glass over Ramana's face, dancing in his eyes. Others come in and take their seats. They begin their hour-and-a-half of sitting still and quietly together. Jonas is filled with gratitude, and takes some time to feel that fully. He looks around him at all these people he hasn't even spoken with but who he feels he knows intimately. Dauriya is sitting next to him with her eyes closed, and she looks radiant, illuminated from within. Clarissa sits calmly, her body very still; George is smiling to himself, and he catches Jonas's eye and smiles at him. He smiles back.

Jonas turns his gaze back to the dais, and he sees that right in the center of the largest bouquet of red and pink roses is one bright yellow one. A lemony fragrance wafts to his nostrils. Here is his offering to D.

Jonas drops into meditation easily, like a pebble into a deep pool falling down, down into the quiet dark.

Jonas is deep in meditation when he sees an image of D appear in his inner vision. It's like there's an HD TV in his mind, the picture is so clear. D is walking toward the meditation hall wearing a red t-shirt and long dark-grey shorts—different from what he wore at breakfast this morning. In a few minutes, Jonas opens his eyes and sees D entering the hall, wearing a red t-shirt and long dark-grey shorts. D takes his place on the dais and sits for five minutes or so until the bell rings that signals the end of meditation.

"Welcome. For our last satsang, I'm going to just open the floor to questions. You may stay in your seat unless you are pulled to come up here."

Jonas's hand shoots up.

"Yes, Jonas." Jonas loves the way D says his name. He sometimes wishes he could record it, so he could play it over and over to himself.

Jonas tells D and the sangha about the vision he just had of D walking to the hall. When he concludes that it was "very cool," D and the sangha laugh aloud. Jonas feels happy.

"Yes, very cool." D smiles at Jonas. "You know, phenomena just appear and disappear. This is true whether seen with the eyes open or closed. It is all just movement and appearance, images on a screen—or on Jonas's inner HD TV." More laughter.

"The appearance of phenomena is ever-changing, and has nothing to do with your unchanging being, your true nature. Phenomena arise out of your conditioning that moves you toward the things you desire, that you think are good for you, and away from the things you fear, that you think are bad for you. Phenomena turn toward you and away from you like the painted horses spinning on a merry-go-round. But there is no movement at all in that which doesn't change. Be still, and you will glimpse who you truly are. And there is more aliveness, more passion, more beauty in that than there are in the painted horses.

"It is all in the mind. Jonas's image of this body walking here is no different. Although he didn't see it with his eyes, the visual sense organ, it is the same. Jonas's image is closer to what is true, however, for it appeared only in his mind. All phenomena are mental projections. Remove time and location, remove subject and object, and the image either disappears altogether or it appears only in the mind that is projecting it."

"Thank you, D," Jonas says.

"You are welcome, Jonas. Very good."

Clarissa has her hand up, and D nods at her.

"D, you may have noticed that my body has stopped jerking around. I feel comfortable in it again. Could you talk a bit about the body, please?"

"Yes, Clarissa, of course. Your body has stopped its involuntary movement because you have stopped resisting. When there is resistance to meeting what you need to, when there is a fear of burning away an obstacle your conditioning has given you, sometimes the body reacts. There might be twitches, there might be pain, or sometimes illness.

"But the body only reacts if you identify with it. You are not your body, just as you are not your mind. Ramana called the body 'alien.' When you are resting in your Self, there are no objects, including the body. When, through self-inquiry, you find the origin of the thoughts that arise, there are no more thoughts. The body, the thoughts, the appearance of phenomena, the separate world of objects, disappears and there is only the one Self. Notice your thoughts as they arise, and find where they come from."

George's hand rises.

"D, I'm a smoker, and I keep trying to quit, but it's hard. I also like to have a drink now and then. Aren't those things bad for my body?"

"George, what's bad for you is identifying with the body. The rest doesn't matter. Smoke, don't smoke; drink, don't drink. Your concern about the body brings your attention to it and causes identification with it. These days there is too much body-identification. Turn your attention to self-inquiry, to finding who you really are. Look for the 'I.' Then what the body is doing and feeling will not matter to you. Turn your attention away from the physical through stillness, through silence. The less attention you give it, the less important it becomes. And the physical phenomenal world begins to wear away. It will recede more and more as your true nature is more and more revealed. This is just the way of it.

"I think it was John in the Christian bible who said something like, 'Do not love the world or the things in the world. If you love the world, you will not know God's love.'"

A meditative quiet pervades the hall. D breathes deeply and closes his eyes. They sit in silence together, breathing together. Eventually, D opens his eyes.

"Is there one more question?"

Brahma's hand is raised, and D nods at him. "Yes, Brahma."

"D, I have such hunger. Such longing. I want to surrender myself completely. I want to attain liberation from the object world, the dream world. I want to be free and resting in what is. I want it so much!" Brahma's eyes well up.

D smiles with familiar affection at Brahma, like a father to his son. Jonas's heart twinges.

"Brahma, your hunger for freedom is beautiful. Yes, surrender and humility are the pathways. And you are humility itself."

D's voice gets even quieter. "But don't make 'reaching enlightenment' a goal. Nurture the intention, but don't desire, for desire will just create attachment and identification with what is false. And don't try to get away from something. Don't run away; don't even run toward. Just be still.

"I know that you, Brahma, like most here, have had many tastes, many openings. But don't dwell on these. Don't try to get that taste again; don't try to 'get' somewhere or 'get' something. Just feel the hunger to be free. Just feel it. It is enough. No goal, no outcome."

D is whispering now, yet his words are easily heard.

"Come out of a place of childlike wonder. Free of any assumption. And fall into this final sweet mystery. The mystery of your Self."

~

In the afternoon, after Jonas has packed and swept out his cottage with a straw broom, he joins the sangha who are clustered in little groups on the grounds. There is a buzz of activity in the air and the chatter of many voices. Suitcases and packs are scattered about. Jonas talks to a few of the sangha members, and Facebook names and email addresses are exchanged. It feels kind of weird to talk with these people in a casual way.

At 3 PM, they all file one last time into the meditation hall, and D says a few words of farewell and gratitude to the sangha and the mountain. He then requests a song from Melanie, a very pretty woman younger than Jonas whose name Jonas didn't know until now. Melanie sits beside D on the dais, closes her eyes, and sings an achingly beautiful song that she wrote about Arunachala. Her voice is the sweetest, purest voice Jonas has ever heard, and her song is poetry and prayer. D has his eyes closed during Melanie's song, and he seems to be in the throes of ecstasy.

After Melanie finishes singing and they all walk out of the meditation hall for the last time, Jonas can't find D anywhere. Jonas doesn't like goodbyes anyway. And he can't imagine how he could possibly say goodbye to this god-man who has given him more than he can say, his own self. He'll see him again. Maybe he'll attend one of the retreats he gives in the States. He says a thank you to D in his heart and takes a rickshaw into Tiru.

Jonas gets a room at Mountain View Towers again—a small room, quite a bit smaller than the one he and Bruce shared, but cheap. He checks in, throws his pack on the bed, and washes his face. He climbs the stairs to the rooftop restaurant, where he first saw Arunachala, and sits on a cushion on the cement floor.

His money is running out. He doesn't have a clue what's next. All he can do is just surrender to the mystery and watch it all unfold.

IV: CONFLUENCES

(Water)

Don't insist on going
where you think you want to go
Ask the way to the spring.

— Rumi, from "Moving Water"

CHAPTER 22

Jonas is standing in a field that stretches as far as his eye can see, without end. Golden grasses move slightly in a breeze so soft he cannot feel it. He starts to walk. The grasses flatten under his feet. His feet are bare and dark brown against the gold of the grass. The sun is hot on his bare back.

He doesn't know how long he's been walking or how far he has walked. How can it be measured? There are no landmarks here. He stands still again. He hears a voice, but doesn't know where it is coming from.

"Where are you?"

Jonas recognizes the voice. So he responds, mouthing the words and letting sound emerge from his lips. "I am here."

"I am here too," is the reply.

Jonas feels an urgency. He scans the field, shielding his eyes from the bright sun. He notices he's wearing bracelets of red-and-orange woven string.

"Where?" Jonas's voice is louder now.

There. A figure appears a long way away, to his left, walking toward him. He smiles and starts walking toward it.

Another figure appears beside the first figure. He looks to his right. There's another figure. And another. He looks around. People are coming toward him from all directions, but he can't see them very well, they are so far away.

He stands still again, confused.

Who are all these people, and why are they walking toward him? They are getting closer. He squints his eyes to see them better. They are wearing different kinds of clothing from other countries, other centuries, from long, heavy, ornate robes to skimpy loincloths; they are men and women, very old and very young, dark-skinned and light-skinned, tall and thin, short and round, a baby crawling through the grass.

That voice, clearly a woman's voice and quite close now, calls to him again.

"Where are you?"

Jonas feels frustrated. There are too many people.

"I am here!"

He realizes with a start that he doesn't know where he is. He wakes up.

Anamika is having a strange day. She feels jittery and distracted and keeps on thinking there's something important she's forgotten to do. Discombobulated. That was a word her mother often used to describe how she was feeling. She used it almost daily in the last year of her life, when her dementia was escalating. "I'm somewhat discombobulated today, dear," she'd say.

Anamika has tried exploring her own "discombobulated" feeling, but keeps coming up against something that's in the way. This is unusual for her. She usually knows, on some level that she can access, what's going on with her. But not this time.

So she keeps herself busy. She goes in to work early, and she and Ramu have time for a chai together before his customers start rolling in. When he asks how her satsangs are going, she tells him how her little place isn't large enough for all of the people to fit in comfortably, and she's not sure what to do about that. She's considering holding them outside, but doesn't know where yet. Does Ramu have any suggestions for her?

Ramu looks like he's thinking. He shuffles some papers around for a few minutes before he speaks.

"Anamika, my friend. You have been good to me and very good for my business. Now my family is very happy because I can buy my wife and children what they desire, such as the beautiful new clothes, and the shiny kitchen gadget for my wife, pretty bangles for my daughter, a new cricket bat for my son. We are even planning to make a holiday to Goa all together!"

"I'm very glad, Ramu."

"How would you like to use these two rooms here for your satsang?" Ramu makes a sweeping motion with his arm, taking in both the front room of the agency, including the desk he sits behind, a couch and several chairs, and the adjoining internet room full of little tables, chairs, and computers. "You would have to hold your satsang in the evenings after I close at 6. And move the furniture as needed. Maybe start at 7 PM?"

"Ramu, are you sure?" Anamika feels something that was out of kilter click into place. "What a wonderful idea, and how very generous of you to offer. What can I give you in return?"

"Anamika!" Ramu waves a finger at her. "I will not accept anything from you. Just keep the place tidy, okay?" He smiles. Anamika rushes over to where Ramu sits behind his desk and hugs him.

He gives her his extra set of keys. "Thank you, Ramu! This will be perfect. I promise to keep everything nice and tidy."

The following day, Anamika is pleased to see Priya return to satsang with her mother. Anamika is outside when they arrive, a little early. Priya has a shy smile on her face when she approaches Anamika, and gives her a very respectful Namaste.

"Anamikaji, after the last satsang with you, I am working on understanding myself and not just thinking about Sudha and feeling the anger about her not trusting me. And now everything is good again! I do not know what is this, what is happening. I did not do anything. Sudha is my very-very good friend again, and I am happy about her marriage to Raj." Priya flashes her stunningly bright smile. "Thank you for showing me what I can do for myself." Anamika gives Priya a little hug.

When everyone is gathered tightly in her little room, Anamika begins to talk.

"When we stop trying to control other people and what we see as 'outside' of us, things change. When we turn our attention to ourselves and see what's there that is creating what is happening, things change. There is no big secret to this. No formula of 'attracting' what we want into our lives. We do it in every moment. What we see, our relationships to each other, what we have in our lives, is all a reflection of our inner landscape which, in turn, is created from our deeply held beliefs and assumptions about ourselves and the world.

"If we think things 'should' be a certain way, and they are not, or we think that others 'should' act a certain way, and they don't, we might get pissed off, irritated, confused, or feel devalued, overwhelmed, depressed. What do we do then? The more we engage with our 'shoulds'—the more we try to artificially impose ourselves upon what's 'out there'—the more helpless and upset we feel.

"Here's the thing: it's already only us out there. If there is a '*secret*,'" Anamika makes air quotes with her fingers, "that's it." She lifts one eyebrow, then laughs conspiratorially.

"But it's not a secret at all; it's very obvious if you're paying attention. For a simple example, one Canadian man walking down the street here might get very irritated at the many beggars who insistently demand rupees, play on his sympathy, and tug aggressively at his clothes. He may explode in anger at the last beggar, the last straw. Another Canadian guy might just smile, happy to be walking down the same street, interacting with the beggars or not. Each man's experience mirrors what's going on within himself; it has nothing to do with what's 'out there.'

"When something feels bad to you, there's the message. It's just like with the body in pain. If there is anger, for example, there is an opportunity for you to look inside and see what's there and where it is coming from. Just the act of looking and exploring, doing the inner work, bringing it back to yourself, is enough to produce change."

Priya nods knowingly.

"It creates a shift. This is where the 'attraction' stuff comes in. There is some truth to this. You do indeed create your reality, of course. This is just a given. It's all about you.

"Interestingly, most of our bad feelings arise from issues around control. Things 'should' be this way, but are out of our control. Or we try and try to make things that way, control the way things go, but fail. Or maybe other people 'should' behave in such-and-such a way to you, to others, to the world in general, and you work to control their behavior—on a personal level, like telling someone not to jump the queue or to litter or to look at other women, or on a societal/global level, like boycotting or protesting.

"What is so interesting about all this is that we are already in the driver's seat, so to speak. Most of us just don't know it. Why? Because we get caught up in our own movie. We get lost in it. We suspend our deep inner knowledge of what is really true. Like children playing house in the backyard. Or building a sandcastle on the beach. We keep ourselves there, playing in the reflection in the water, and don't turn toward the source of the reflection.

"And, oh, we have many means of distracting ourselves from ourselves, don't we? Lots of shiny things."

A British voice from the back of the room asks, "Such as mobiles?"

Another chimes in. "Anything from Apple!"

"Yup, there's all that, of course. They are especially good at taking us out of the here and now, the present moment, to some imagined future place and person. In a way, social media reveals how reality is truly imagined. It peels away the veneer of physical reality, the 'hard matter' stuff, and reveals that it's solely about relationships. When you're on the bus texting someone on your phone about meeting up that evening, the people around you on the bus, and the bus itself, disappear from your attention, and you are engaging only with words on a screen from a person who is not there about some future event that doesn't exist and might never exist!"

Some people chuckle.

"It's all very insubstantial, isn't it? Tenuous. It exists only in the imagination."

Bruce says, "Remember that old Temptations song?" He sings the song's title, "Just My Imagination (Running Away With Me)." A few people join in. Someone drums a rhythm on the floor, and the song gets taken up by more people. Most of the group are now singing, moving their heads in time. After a couple of minutes, it winds up in laughter.

"So," Anamika speaks softly, after the song and laughter have died down. "I'd like to finish early today. I think that was a good way to end." She pauses, and frowns slightly.

"I have a confession. The subject of my talk today really came out of how I'm feeling—which is a bit out of sorts. And, personally, I need to do some checking out of what's going on. That's why I want to cut this short. Hope you understand."

She gives them the news about their new meeting place, upstairs in Ramu's Travel, and hopes they can come in the evenings from now on, at 7 PM. She will set up a schedule that will be on the notice board in the agency.

CHAPTER 23

There are too many people in Tiru. And too many honking cars and rickshaws. Too many Indians wanting something from him, usually money or "just looking" in their shops. There's "too much of a muchness," Jonas thinks, recalling the phrase from, what... *Alice in Wonderland*. That would be appropriate. Being here in India is kind of like being down the rabbit hole. Crazy, magical, mysterious. Nonsensical.

And it's strange to see all of these foreigners he doesn't know, healthy-looking white people roaming the streets, sitting in restaurants. He's used to being with the same group of people, the sangha, day in and out. And all of the notices everywhere advertising various satsangs and spiritual stuff—which he's not interested in anymore. Not that he ever really was. Even in Ramana's ashram there are too many people milling about. But at least they are quiet. So he spends time meditating there. And as soon as he leaves the grounds, there's the noisy, chaotic world again.

What to do, as they say in India. What to do.

For a few days after the retreat, Jonas did as little as possible. But now he's beginning to feel anxious. There's some fear tattering the edges of his consciousness. Shouldn't he be making plans of some kind? The departure date on his ticket is for six weeks away. When he bought the ticket he didn't know that he was going to spend most of his money on a retreat with a guru. So now he has time but no money. Maybe he can do some travel close by, on the cheap? Go to a beach. He's heard of a beach by Auroville, the planned utopian community on the outskirts of Pondicherry, and another one in Mamallapuram, where there are some famous temples and ancient carvings. Neither is far from here, a few hours in a bumpy cab or crowded bus, close to Chennai. Then what. Change his ticket and go home early? Then what. Find work?

What to do.

Ah, but now he's too much in his head. That was the problem. That was where the fear came in. He needed to keep centered inside, be in the moment, empty his head. Breathe. Trust. Feel D in his heart.

So Jonas takes a walk. A walking meditation. He walks out of town, and keeps on walking, sticking close to the edge of the road, as far from traffic as possible, ignoring rickshaw drivers who stop to ask if he needs a ride. He walks until he leaves the main town; he walks along a street full of temples where orange-robed, long-bearded sadhus sit and smoke on the side of the road; he walks along a street lined with little hole-in-the-wall restaurants, and tiny shops with glassed-in shelves of colorful orange and yellow sweets, and chai stalls where Indian men stand around and chat, holding little steaming cups in their hands. He finds himself outside that travel agency he'd visited before, Ramu's Travel. Maybe he'll check out the cost of fares to Mamallapuram. He walks in.

There, lounging comfortably with a book on an old couch in the front room, is Bruce.

~

Anamika closes her eyes and she is by a river that runs through a field of golden grass. She hears the river rushing and feels its cool air brush her bare arms. The river invites her. She walks into the river so that she is ankle-deep in the cold water. She listens carefully. This is what it says.

There are many points of confluence
where tide meets river;
sometimes the water
flows backward into eddies.

These are places of power.

If you stand in this place
you will see the points
of your lives swirling around your feet.

Splash the water on your face
with a cupped hand and feel its coolness.

There are many lifetimes held
in one drop of water
and the song that sings itself
is in each one, each drop of grace.

Anamika bends down and with cupped hands splashes the river water on her face. The drops roll down over her closed eyes, and in one of them she sees Jonas.

"Well, well," Jonas speaks softly, staring at Bruce. He feels something that was out of kilter click into place.

"Well, well," he speaks again, more loudly this time. Bruce still doesn't look up from his book.

"Bruce, man!"

Bruce starts. "Jonas!" He leaps off the couch and gives him a big bear hug. "Good to see you!"

"Good to see *you*! I wasn't sure that was going to happen again."

"I guess the retreat's over, huh?" Bruce searches Jonas's face.

"Yeah. So, why did you leave Ramana's ashram? What's going on?"

Bruce has a wide grin on his tanned face. "That's what's going on," he says and points to a slight woman with long dark curly hair in a gold and green salwar kameez who's leaning over a computer table in the adjoining internet room, talking to someone.

Jonas laughs and is about to nudge Bruce and say something like "What else is new?" when the woman straightens up suddenly and looks right at Jonas.

Jonas is immediately flooded in recognition. His whole body is awash in electric tingles.

Anamika walks over to Jonas and Bruce, not leaving Jonas's eyes for a moment. Bruce looks from Jonas to Anamika and back to Jonas.

"Uh, do you guys know each other?"

Anamika extends her hand to Jonas.

"Hi! I'm Anamika."

Jonas knows that voice.

She is here. He is here too.

Anamika's ears are filled with a rushing sound. She recognizes Jonas as a partner self, another incarnation of her whole Self, one of many she knows of and has communicated with on different levels of consciousness. But she's not very interested in the particulars of these other lives, and she is fuzzy on time-space frames; she wasn't aware that this one was here and now. And there was something about this one, too. Something that called to her. Or were they calling to each other?

She feels a loosening inside, as if she used to be in a rowboat that was tethered by a rope to a tree on the riverbank, and now the knot in the rope has come undone and she is floating down the river in her boat, with no paddles. Before, she could see where she was in relationship to everything around her. Now everything is moving, shifting, and she is being carried by the river, going who-knows-where, watching the familiar riverbanks recede as she's carried further downstream. All she can do is go with it. Life is but a dream.

It's time for Anamika's lunch break, and she suggests Jonas and Bruce walk down the street with her to a little paratha stand. They walk quietly. Bruce looks like he is using as much restraint as he can muster, though it's evident he is bursting with curiosity. Anamika and Jonas say very little. Although they keep glancing at each other, they haven't exchanged words other than that first "Hi."

They sit together at the paratha stand, around a small table in the street, and order paratha and bottles of water.

"So, what's going on with you two? Do you know each other?" Bruce looks from Anamika to Jonas. "Jonas?"

Jonas keeps his gaze fixed on Anamika.

"I'm not sure," Jonas finally responds. "I feel like I do. I don't think we've ever met. But we've spoken together before, I'm sure of it."

"Did you call the travel agency? Sometimes Anamika answers the phone if Ramu's away," Bruce offers helpfully.

"No, I don't mean in that way. I mean, like, in my head."

Anamika talks to Jonas directly for the first time. "Yes, we have communicated before, in different ways." She smiles warmly at Jonas, and her face lights up. "I didn't expect to see you here in front of me, though."

Anamika likes Jonas's dark eyes and long hair. There is something almost childlike in the lankiness of his body and in his sweet yet serious face. She lets herself feel the joy of this wondrous meeting. How cool is this.

Bruce nods his head slowly, as he begins to understand. Jonas is transfixed by Anamika—her open smile, her almond eyes that he's sure he's seen before, and of course her voice.

"Jonas, Anamikaji is my guru. She gives satsangs here."

Jonas takes a deep breath and lets it out slowly.

"Whew. Wow." He gathers his thoughts and then lets them go. A smile grows on his face. "How friggin' cool is this!"

After Anamika returns to work, Bruce and Jonas take a rickshaw into Tiru and have chai together in the rooftop restaurant of Mountain View Towers. They have a lot to catch up on. Jonas tells him about D and the retreat and some of the experiences he had there: his name on the mountain, the inner vision of D walking to the meditation hall, and the hours of tasting enlightenment when his head cracked open. Bruce reacts enthusiastically, and Jonas is grateful, happy to be understood and back in the comfortable place of their friendship. In return, Bruce tells him about Anamika and tries to summarize the gist of her teachings and exercises as well as he can.

Jonas is thoughtful as Bruce is explaining, and chooses his words carefully. "I think I get some of what you're saying. But it's quite different from what I know to be true. With D, I mean."

"Yeah, I know. Different from Ramana's teachings. But maybe not as different as you think. I thought some of it was way out there at first, you know? But the more I listened, the more it made sense. And the exercise-type-things she has us do—they bring it all into your body, your bones, where you can feel the truth of it." Bruce pauses, and grins. "Besides, there's something about this girl."

"Yes. Definitely with you there."

"And, hey. Those poems you channeled back in Vancouver. That voice you heard in your head." Bruce raises his eyebrows. "Anamika?"

"Could be. Yeah. Wild, huh." Jonas lights a cigarette, takes a long drag, and exhales. "There's been more, too. When I was on retreat. More poems, and some prose about a guitar maker. And a couple of dreams. Writing, too. A different kind of writing than the poems. It sounds like what you said you were doing with her. Life interpretation stuff. But D talked about that, too. You know, symbols. Stuff like that."

No one talks for a while. Jonas smokes his cigarette and gazes at Arunachala. Bruce stirs more sugar into his chai.

"So, uh. Is she just your guru? Or…?" Jonas keeps his eyes on the mountain.

Bruce looks carefully at Jonas's profile, and clears his throat. "I don't know. We've slept together a couple of times."

Jonas looks at Bruce. "Yeah. I'm not surprised."

"I don't know what it meant." Bruce stares into his chai. "If it meant anything to her."

"Really."

"But it did to me."

Jonas looks up at the mountain.

"Jonas, I think I love her."

Jonas turns so he is facing Bruce all the way. "You know, Bruce, it's common for people to fall in love with their gurus. It's part of the process. It happened to me. And D's a he! Maybe it's like that?"

"Maybe." Bruce groans a little. "Man, I dunno. Who's to say anything about love? I don't know if there's one kind and another or if it's all the same. But there is a sexual element there for me, for sure."

Jonas turns back to face the mountain. They sit together in silence, sipping their chai and gazing at Arunachala.

CHAPTER 24

Anamika rips a piece of paper out of her notebook, draws a big arrow pointing up, writes "Ramu's Travel, satsang 7 PM," and tapes it outside her door.

She is getting ready for her first satsang at Ramu's agency. She has decided that the bigger computer room is the best place for it, so she pushes the tables with the computers on them to the edges of the room, fiddles with the wires and cables so that they are out of the way, and groups the chairs together in the newly opened space. There is about twice as much space here as she had in her room. It looks like it's going to work.

People start to come in around 6:40, and mill around. A few of the older people sit on the chairs. Some are hanging out on the couch in the adjoining room. There are more people than before. Anamika is still surprised that people come at all. People put so much trust in her without even knowing why. They listen to what she says; they do what she tells them to do. It's a responsibility that Anamika takes very seriously. She is in awe of it.

And there's Jonas and Bruce, walking in together. Anamika feels something akin to butterflies in her tummy. Is she nervous? About what? As everyone files into the computer room, she takes her seat, closes her eyes, and goes inside for a few moments. The room settles and grows calm.

"Welcome to satsang. And welcome to our new space. I have a schedule posted on Ramu's notice board. We'll be holding satsang twice a week now." Anamika looks at the many faces gathered in a semi-circle around her, and is again struck with gratitude.

"Thank you for coming to see me. I respect and honor the trust you show in me. Oh, and I want to thank you for leaving me such lovely gifts—and rupees!—last time. It was such a sweet surprise. So, in the spirit of that, I now have a plate on that table over there, if you'd like to leave something in exchange for what you feel you've received here. Whatever you like, and only if you want to." Anamika puts her palms together in Namaste, and the group follows suit.

"Let's begin by just being quiet and still together for about ten minutes or so. Close your eyes if you like, and let's just go inside for a while. This time, let's not look for anything, but just notice. And notice how when you notice something, it then disappears. Watch whatever is there—your thoughts, feelings, aches and pains—pass by like clouds in the sky. Like leaves on a river."

When the meditation is over, Anamika takes in the people in the room. She is completely present and calm in her body now, and her senses are open, attuned to the energy of the beings around her. The topic of her talk comes to her out of the middle of the room, the center of a web of bright, interconnected lines of sparking electrical energy. And she speaks.

"I'd like to talk this evening about karma—cause and effect. Much is made of karma in eastern religions. The philosophy or assumption is that you come into this life with karma from your past lives, and it shows in your life in different ways—in traditional Hinduism, through caste and status in the community, for example. The higher your caste, the less bad karma you have. And once your karma is worked out, you can get off the treadmill of reincarnation and attain enlightenment and peace. In the West, we see it as something like the biblical

'You reap what you sow' notion. Or there's that Paul Butterfield song my mother used to sing, 'It All Comes Back.'

"Popular mainstream science appears to confirm the philosophy of karmic cause and effect in the physical world. You know the common saying, for every action, there's a reaction? That's the simplistic—and incorrect, by the way—interpretation of Newton's third law, which is really about something different. My apologies to Newton. But the point here is, for most of us in the West and East, cause and effect seems like a done deal. An irrefutable fact.

"The widespread belief goes like this: For every cause there's an effect, and this plays out in one's life. So if you do good, you get good in return. Do bad, you get bad. If it doesn't look like it's happening that way, us Westerners seem to trust that it will eventually play out. We say stuff like 'Karma will get him' or 'Karma's a bitch.' It makes us feel better, right? That there's a simple equation: this equals that. That there's some overriding *fairness* in life.

"None of it is true."

Some uncomfortable shifting has been occurring during her speech. An older Indian man she hasn't seen before, and who had been sitting on a chair in the back, gets up abruptly and leaves. A few heads turn to watch. Anamika swallows. Has she finally hit on something that will elicit the anger she experienced in Vancouver? She's already covered so much ground here in her satsangs, and conveyed stuff that many people back home just didn't want to hear and reacted to badly. It's been going so well, so smoothly. Is "karma" going to interrupt her easy streak? Anamika's butterflies return.

Should she remind the group that she's not speaking from any tradition? And that while she respects all traditions, she will likely say stuff that contradicts them? And maybe piss people off? No, she decides. This is her satsang. The people come here to learn what she knows. No qualification, no apology. She continues.

"Let's take a look at the notion of 'fairness.' What's fair to you? Let's say that your partner cheated on you. You've been nothing but a loving, giving husband, and you find out that your wife has been lying to you for months and sleeping with your best friend. You've been unfairly treated, betrayed. Or maybe that's too complex an example, there are too many factors involved. Some of you here might even have been the cheater: you've fallen helplessly in love with someone else and don't want to hurt your spouse, so you hide it. Or you have an affair to end your marriage that you weren't happy in anymore, whether you do it consciously or not. Okay. Forget that one. Say you've been the victim of ongoing physical and sexual abuse by your father. Hmmm… Again, maybe not a good example. We know that those who victimize others usually do so out of their own pain, because they've been victimized in similar ways themselves. The cycle of abuse continues. Okay. I'll try again. Let's say that someone does something unspeakably and intentionally bad. Any ideas?"

"How about murder?" Maryam suggests. "Someone murders your sister. Rapes her and murders her."

Someone pipes up. "Yeah, but the rapist-murderer is probably fucked up, right? No happy person does that kind of thing. He's in pain, too, whether he knows it or not. People aren't bad, they're just hurt. And, you know, hurt people hurt people."

Kris adds, "We all do what we need to. We create our own world out of our beliefs and assumptions. It reflects ourselves back to us."

"Okay," Anamika smiles. "True enough. Thanks, guys. But let's explore the common notion of karma here. The victim's family probably isn't thinking about the criminal's psychological make-up or tragic personal history. And let's say the criminal isn't charged for the crime, so it's very unjust. He walks away free. Laughing. The victim's family is enraged and, of course, in terrible grief. It's so unfair. They feel victimized all over again. So they want very much to believe that since justice wasn't reached in court, the criminal will get his own, somehow, somewhere. Karma will look after it. They want him to experience their great pain—understand and feel what he put them through. He deserves it."

Anamika pauses. "Is this somewhat accurate, do you think? I'm not very good at talking about this kind of stuff because it doesn't really exist in this way. It's all imaginary, living art, created by the people in the story. But I'm trying to see it as I think others generally do, even though it's just not really what's going on."

"Yeah," Bruce speaks up. "You're doing just fine with the common-perception thing. But, Anamikaji, the murderer can't ever experience his victims' pain because he is not them. He lives in his own separate, self-constructed world. Uncommonly speaking, that is!"

Anamika laughs. "I can't get very far with this line of thought because you guys rightly shut it down! You've learned well.

"Okay, let's try this. Imagine that each person in the world has, in a lifetime, exactly the same amount of happiness and pain as the next person. I'm not saying it's true necessarily, but just imagine it. If you really understood that everyone has exactly the same amount of happiness and pain, then maybe you wouldn't feel unfairly treated, envious, or victimized. You wouldn't need to take revenge or seek justice. You wouldn't be concerned about whether your sister's rapist-murderer will get his due in one way or another. You wouldn't be concerned about whether your ex-wife will ever feel what you felt when she left you. You wouldn't need to wipe that smile off of anyone's face."

The room quiets down as people contemplate this.

Jonas, however, has been fidgeting a bit, and now speaks up. "Anamika, I don't mean any disrespect. But aren't we talking about free will now? If what I or anyone else did had nothing to do with my happiness or pain, I wouldn't need to do anything. It's all already looked after. Pre-ordained. Divinely orchestrated. I can just surrender. 'Thy will be done.'"

Anamika realizes that she has opened the flood-gates to arguments on ethics, free will, self-determination, destiny. She feels suddenly tired. Maybe 7 PM satsangs aren't going to work.

"Thanks, Jonas. Yes, maybe I was. Touching on free will, that is. Or not. I'll try to address this. Give me a moment." Anamika closes her eyes and breathes deeply.

"The end of a life isn't a punishment, of course; it isn't a terrible thing. Just as we each choose our parents and the circumstances of our birth—'we' being our greater Selves *and* the individual personality—we also choose how and when we will die. Each length of a life is perfect, whole, complete to the person who lives it. Longer isn't better. Size doesn't matter. You often hear people talk about 'what a waste' it is when a talented person dies young, as if, if they had lived just a little longer, they would have 'given the world' something great—usually in the arts or sciences. 'Think of all the great music he would have composed if he'd lived longer, and now we'll never get to hear it. What a waste!' Or 'She might have found the cure for cancer had she lived. What a waste!'

"There is no waste, however. Nothing, nobody is cut short before their time. There are no possible future achievements that death cuts down before they are realized. That's a misconception about time as well as an assumption about how long a life should be. It's all perfect as it is. And it all, finally, makes perfect sense to the individual because it's his life and he lives and dies as he wants to. As he needs to. His adventure is over when he has completed it, no matter what kind of 'time' it takes to fulfill his unique, private purposes. Who are we to say otherwise? We try not to judge how a life is lived by another; why do we judge its length?

"Free will or destiny? Both? Because the kind of choosing I'm talking about doesn't take place in the individual conscious mind; it's not a decision that you make and then use your will to enact. There is trust involved. Trust that you know what you're doing on a greater level. That it does or will make sense if you can see it clearly, see the big picture. Trust that everything that happens is indeed all okay. That it is...meant to be. Aha! Maybe the 'free will vs. destiny' categories themselves are just more erroneous polarities! Sort of like 'cause and effect.' Or 'positive and negative.' You decide. I think I'm getting off-track here, in any case."

There are too many possible paths to take, too many tracks off to the side to wander down. Anamika feels awkward, even nervous. Those butterflies. Is Jonas's presence here changing something in her?

Anamika closes her eyes, takes a deep breath, and opens her inner senses. She hears the sound of water and sees a small spring trickling from dry earth. She opens her eyes and takes a sip from the water bottle next to her chair. And this time her words come forth as easily as water from a spring.

"What I'm about to say isn't meant to imply that, if you're so inclined, you should stop fighting political oppression and social injustice, or stop saving the environment, stop giving to charity and 'helping' others any way you can. Like everything in the social-political arena, these 'battles' have always existed and always will—as long as there are people who believe there is something to fight for. Participate in them or not. Though one could say that participating in them merely maintains and prolongs the conditions of divisiveness, the 'us and them.'

"And these battles aren't really what they seem. The purpose of political activism and the results of 'helping' are not as objective and clear as you think. We all want to help, don't we? And we all know examples where our help has had a very different effect than what we aimed for—whether it's one person 'helping' another, or one country 'helping' another. What is helping, anyway? How can we help others? Why do we do it?

"The people who get actively involved in social-political change really do so because they need to—to fulfill a personal purpose. And usually this purpose is not evident to them. So they project it outside of themselves. As their exterior drama unfolds they participate in it passionately, fighting for their causes and not noticing the arrogance in their assumptions that they know what's best for everyone. That they know how to help.

"What you do and the effects it has is not a simple equation.

"You can have no idea of the effects of your actions on others. You can't even imagine. It's just not possible. Even if you kill someone, you don't know what you've done to her or to her family. It's presumptuous to think that you do.

"On another, deeper, level, *you* haven't done anything *to* them at all. The murder of your sister, say, exists in your life in the way that you have it there. It is a part of your life canvas, and you have made the brush strokes. No one really does anything to anyone else. You may feel hurt, feel pain, feel anger—that's you again, still. Your feelings. They originate in you, like a spring bubbling forth from the earth. Your emotions move through you. And they create their own effects. In your body, your perceptions, your behavior, your world. In you. There is only you.

"I think it was our main man himself, Ramana, who, when asked, 'How can we help others?' replied, 'There are no others.'

"You cause everything that you see in your world. Period. And your world is the effect."

Anamika ends the satsang rather abruptly, without an exercise or a meditation. As the people walk out, she hears a few raised voices, bits of argumentative-sounding discussions. And she sees some people drop rupees onto the plate. Bruce and Jonas hang back.

"Wow, that was different from what I expected," Jonas says quietly to Bruce. "Those examples she gave. Pretty extreme. I get what she was saying, but bringing in politics? I can see how that could be…what. Controversial."

To Jonas's mild chagrin, it looks like Anamika has overheard him. As she walks toward them, she says brightly, "I agree completely!"

Bruce smiles at her affectionately. "Yeah, I feel like it was kind of different than usual tonight, Anamika. Still good, though!"

"It was really interesting," Jonas adds quickly.

They help her put the computer tables and chairs back the way they were, and Bruce asks Anamika over for a late dinner. She looks questioningly at Jonas.

"I'll be there, too. Bruce is my roomie again! Or, I'm his, I guess."

"That's great. So, you're in the 'hood."

"Yes, indeed. And it's way cheaper than where I used to be at the hotel. I'm grateful to my old pal here. I was getting down to the wire, money-wise. Good thing he's got a pretty big place!" Jonas gives Bruce a friendly slap on the back. Something about Bruce makes Jonas do macho things that normally he wouldn't.

Anamika collects her donation plate and rupees, and the three of them walk side by side to Bruce's apartment, with Anamika in the middle. There's a light breeze in the night air, and Jonas is feeling good. Things change quickly here. Just a couple of days ago, he thought he'd never see Bruce again, and had no idea what he was going to do. And now he's not only hanging out with Bruce, but also with someone who is very important to him in ways he can't understand just yet. But he's looking forward to finding out.

They all seem happy and light as they walk down the road. Anamika puts a hand in the crook of each of their elbows. "Look at us. Three Vancouverites walking down a dirt road in India together! At the foot of the holy mountain." Jonas can smell her hair. Coconut oil. He feels a pang in his stomach. He must be hungry, he thinks.

Bruce and Jonas have planned this dinner, and have done some serious shopping. They have samosas, paratha, and dal all ready to eat. Barfi and bananas for dessert. And even a few large bottles of Kingfisher beer.

"Wowee! Beer! What a treat," Anamika exclaims. "Where did you find it?"

"We haff our vays, Fraulein," Bruce says in a bad German accent, while Jonas cracks open a bottle. They toast to meeting each other. The beer slides satisfyingly cold and golden down Jonas's throat and sets a small warm fire in his belly. So good, this familiar feeling: drinking beer with friends. It feels like the three of them could be anywhere—a house party in Vancouver maybe. They toast to India. They toast to Canada. They toast to Arunachala. They eat and drink and talk for hours about this and that, and it feels like home. It feels like they've taken a holiday from India. A holiday from the holy days. Jonas needed this.

Sometime after midnight, Bruce falls asleep. The food has all been eaten, and the beer is almost gone. All that's left is what's in their glasses. Jonas is feeling a bit drunk. Anamika looks sober, but Jonas knows she couldn't be: she drank as much as he did, and she's half his size.

The conversation turns personal. Jonas learns that neither of them have siblings. And that Anamika's parents divorced when she was nine, and she was raised by her actress-teacher mother who died recently and who had dementia, and he tells Anamika about his research-scientist mother dying of cancer when he was less than three, barely in his memory, and being raised by a single businessman father who had a steady stream of girlfriends. He tells her about the abrupt end to his college teaching career and his marriage, his life falling apart, and how it brought him here, and to finding his guru, D. And the poems that brought him here, too.

He tells her about the first time he heard a voice ask where he was, and about the words that spilled from his pen without his awareness. He tells her about doing a writing exercise that was given in a dream. And, in a tipsy attempt to summarize, he tells her that what D gives him and what he gets from this other stuff seem quite different, and he doesn't know what to think about that.

Then he looks hard at Anamika. "Who are you?" he asks, and as he puts his elbow on the table to lean in closer, he knocks over his glass of beer.

"Oh, shit." He and Anamika jump back from the table as the beer runs like a little waterfall over the edge of it.

Anamika laughs. "Jonas, let's talk more tomorrow. I can answer your question then. I think I better be going home now."

Jonas is wiping up with napkins. "Good idea. But let me walk you home. I insist."

They are mostly quiet as they walk the ten minutes to Anamika's place, passing by sleeping figures here and there on the side of the road. Jonas's head is spinning, a combination of alcohol and Anamika, he thinks. They arrive at her door and hug goodbye. Jonas is a lot taller than she is, and he bends down to hug her. His head is over hers and the scent of coconut fills his nostrils deliciously. He draws his head closer, buries his face in her long curly hair, and breathes deeply. Her hair tickles his nose. She moves her head away, tilts it up, and looks at him, studying his face. Her face is shining and intensely familiar, and he thinks he's in a dream. She's the most magically beautiful woman he's ever seen. He wants to walk into her dark almond eyes.

He brings his mouth to hers, and they meet. A few strands of her hair are caught between their lips, and he moves his mouth away for a moment and gently brushes her hair aside. They kiss again.

"Right." Jonas steps away. "See you tomorrow. I'll come by, okay?"

"Yup, tomorrow. 'Night. Thanks for the evening." Anamika closes the door behind her, and Jonas walks back home, to the new place that Bruce has welcomed him into. Jonas feels intermittently happy and sick to his stomach.

CHAPTER 25

Jonas wakes up with a hangover. It's late in the morning. He looks at his travel clock. 11:11. Bruce isn't here; he must have gone out. Jonas wonders where he went. What a night. Jonas takes a shower, throwing buckets of cold water over his head and body. It feels good and bad, satisfying, like he's doing penance. Afterward, he looks at himself in the mirror. Runs his hand over his face. Should he shave? He has lots of dark stubble. Scruff. Maybe he should grow a beard. Maybe he'd look more like D that way.

God, he misses D. It's like he was in this amazing, all-consuming love relationship, and suddenly it's over. Does D think of him? How can he love a man this much? Did he love his father this much? Did his father love him this way? Does he?

He stumbles out of the little washroom back to his mattress on the floor, and sits in a half-lotus upon it. He brings D's image into his mind, and is immediately filled with warmth and comfort. He imagines his smile. The intimacy he felt in his presence.

D, what's going on with me now? His life seems to be spinning wildly. Such a contrast from the peaceful retreat, the days filled with revelation that unfolded slowly or suddenly but that all made sense somehow with D's guidance. Now, here, it's all coming on too fast. And he doesn't understand any of it. Bruce,

Anamika. What happened last night? They talked…and kissed. Shit. Bruce is in love with her. And he kissed her. But there's something there, obviously enough, between them. Bruce knows that. But Bruce is his friend, probably his best friend in the world. Fuck. What has he done.

He wishes he could talk to D. Where's satsang when you need it? So he falls into meditation (what else can he do?) and when he's in it, he talks to D. Or he imagines he talks to D.

D tells him to experience his feelings. To go into them, without the story attached.

Jonas falls into his feelings. There's desire: for Anamika as a woman, and for understanding their connection. There's guilt: for wanting to know her even though Bruce has feelings for her. And fear: of finding out what exactly their relationship is. And of Bruce's reaction, of hurting him. And anticipation: for where it all might lead.

But this is all story, Jonas. Feel the feelings without the story attached.

An image of Sebastian appears, pleading with Jonas, asking Jonas to forgive him, that he couldn't help loving Carla, they couldn't help falling in love, that he valued his friendship. And Jonas acknowledges him for the first time. He doesn't turn away. He feels something that may be forgiveness, or at least a glimmer of understanding. God, Sebastian. You fucker. My friend. My friend.

He feels like he's crawled inside of Sebastian, and into his pain. He had no idea Seb had any pain. And then it breaks open, and it's Jonas's pain. And it is a red river that flows through his body and gathers in a lake in the center of his chest, and it is fire and it hurts. And it is burning in his body everywhere, and he is brave enough to just let it burn. And stays with it while it's burning, not knowing if there'll be anything of him left.

The story has fallen away. And Jonas's face is flushed bright red where he sits in a half-lotus on the mattress on the floor. And it is wet, covered in tears.

~

As Jonas walks to Anamika's place, he feels as if he has been emptied, cleaned right out, and he is just a hollow reed where only his breath passes freely through, unencumbered. It feels great.

Jonas arrives on Anamika's doorstep, and before he can knock she opens the door.

"Jonas! Hello." Anamika's eyes shine, and they are all Jonas can see. "I was just going out. Join me?"

Jonas climbs on the back of Anamika's scooter and they drive for a while. They drive past the ashram where Jonas went on retreat. It surprises him that it still exists. That it has a life independent of his experience there, independent of D. He watches it pass by longingly. The roads get increasingly unfamiliar. Anamika parks the scooter on an out-of-the-way dirt road outside of a tiny restaurant. Jonas is disappointed the ride has ended. He was enjoying sharing a scooter seat with her and watching India fly by.

"I like to come here for eggs. Sometimes they have chicken too, which is pretty much illegal or something. Shhhh… Don't tell anyone! Wouldn't want my friends here to get in trouble." As Anamika and Jonas walk in, Anamika is greeted effusively by a middle-aged man who immediately calls over his shoulder to his wife who comes out from the back, wiping chapati flour off her hands.

"Akash, Deepa, this is my friend, Jonas. He's from Canada, too—so you don't have to ask him that question!" Anamika hugs Deepa and shakes Akash's hand warmly.

"You are knowing us too well, Anamika," Deepa laughs heartily. "Sit-sit."

Once they are seated, Akash and Deepa embark upon the litany of friendly, probing questions Indians commonly ask foreigners, only minus the "what country?" one: "What job?" "Wife?" "Children?" "Why not?" Jonas politely responds with his usual difficulty until Anamika, obviously sensing his discomfort as he tries to answer why not, interrupts them and orders her "usual" for them both.

It's the tastiest masala omelet Jonas has ever eaten, thick, dense, and spicy, with little bits of vegetables adding color and crunch. And surrounding it are chunks of fried potato that are crispy brown on the outside, as well as an oily, buttery mess of onions, tomatoes, and green peppers. If he were still feeling hungover, this would be perfect hangover food.

"Are you hungover Anamika?"

"A little bit."

Jonas likes the way she says this, the way her lips form the words and stay a bit open after the last one. He kissed those lips last night. "I woke up feeling crappy, but then something very cool happened. Or, maybe I should say very 'hot.'"

Anamika raises one eyebrow. "Tell me about it?"

And Jonas tells her about the burning. And how he felt he was going to burn up completely. But that he stayed with it and let it burn.

For context, he tells her about D's teaching: that as the "character" unravels and gets closer to disappearing into the true Self, one experiences the burning away of issues that have arisen from one's conditioning. He describes how conditioning from a very young age creates the layers of the egoic shell that act as armor, ostensibly protecting the character, or the personality, from feeling pain while paradoxically also causing separation and preventing one from realizing one's true nature. And that by feeling into the pain and burning away the issues, the layers of the shell become thinner, and the character ripens, becomes more ready for dissolving into the bliss of the eternal Self. And once you meet your issues, burn them away, they are gone forever. They don't come up in the world anymore because you've seen into what they are, which is fantasy—like the monsters under the bed that the child is scared of until she is brave enough to take a good look. He adds that he didn't know until his experience this morning that what D was talking about was actual physical-feeling burning!

He hopes he doesn't sound too much like a nerd as he's describing this. D's way with words was sometimes quite abstract and intellectual, which always resonated with Jonas. But from what he heard from Anamika in satsang, she herself was no intellectual slouch.

"Interesting. So, the issues that you acquire through conditioning that form the protective shell of ego—if I have this correctly—are they like karma?"

"Yeah, I think so. Some people have a heavier karmic load than others, D says. Could be from a past life. But he also says that all that doesn't matter and that you can wake up in an instant!" Jonas snaps his fingers like D.

Then he suddenly remembers the subject of Anamika's talk in satsang: karma. "Um, I guess this doesn't ring true for you?"

"If it's true for you, it's true enough for me," Anamika responds, rather enigmatically Jonas thinks.

There are a couple of minutes of silence.

"So. Anamika. I have some questions, as you know. Burning questions, you could say!"

Jonas looks around the little restaurant and decides they can talk without interruption. And there's much he wants to ask her.

"Shoot. But, Jonas, before you begin, do you happen to have a smoke?"

Jonas grins and pulls out his pack of Marlboros. They order chai and bottles of water and settle in for their talk, smoking cigarettes. It's been a long time since Jonas felt this comfortable with a woman. He still feels like a hollow reed, an open channel, open to anything.

～

"So. Anamika. I'll try this again sober. Who are you? And who are we to each other?"

Anamika tells him about partner selves that inhabit the same greater Self, like aspects or characteristics of one personality, only they are independent beings that exist in different time periods or geographical locations or even dimensions. She uses the finger-hand analogy that she used in satsang. "We are two fingers on the same hand. Co-incarnations, if you like."

"Well. Wow." Jonas takes this in, and it makes perfect sense to him in the moment. A strange kind of sense. He asks her about the voice and the writing and the dreams. Although he feels like he already knows what she'll say. The last time—well, the only time—he felt this kind of recognition and deep understanding was with D.

"I think partner selves communicate on some level all the time. And it's just a matter of tuning in to where that communication is going on, like tuning in to another frequency. I can do that consciously, and pretty much at will, and so I check in with my partner selves if I want to—as a way of checking in with myself, the wholeness of myself. It's the same thing as you expressing potential abilities or talents you find in yourself. For example, in later life you might learn to, say, draw or paint because you've always felt a slight attraction to it, and it's been getting stronger. When you splash paint on the canvas or sketch on your pad, you are in communion with a partner self whose job in another century may be painting likenesses of a royal family. There is constant sharing going on, and the arts is an easy place to recognize that, and to connect, because it's a creative, exploratory, non-mental space. An alternate reality. Dreams are good for that, too."

"Maybe," Jonas interjects, "and correct me if I'm wrong—but maybe this breakdown of everything in my life that I knew and thought I could count on as secure and solid, maybe that breakdown opened some door...to you? Because when I first heard this clear voice ask me where I was, I felt like I was drowning. And right after that was the first time a poem came." Jonas thinks of D and smiles. "D would say the breakdown was a gift, and the voice and poem, an offering of grace."

"Yes! Breakdowns literally break down old modes of perception, break them apart. In that way you can walk right through them. As for 'grace,' and 'gift,'" Anamika makes little air quotes with her fingers, "I don't use those words because

I don't see things in those terms, those metaphors. To me they indicate something apart from myself. And I don't see anything as apart from myself."

"And Lars the Luthier…?"

"That was the writing about the guitar maker, right? Jonas, do you play guitar or another instrument?"

"Guitar, yeah, a little. Oh, I see." It wasn't just fiction. And it wasn't just some dude from long ago somehow telling him his story. It had something to do with him. It was a part of *him.* "So, do you contact Lars too?"

"Can't say I have. But that doesn't matter. Maybe I will someday. Or maybe he's an aspect of you that's separate from me. You, too, have your own independence."

"What?" Jonas is reminded of his dream and the hundreds of people coming toward him. "Is there no limit?" He has a sense of himself expanding, growing physically larger, huge, without end. Then there is a stab of fear and he is suddenly overwhelmed and small again. Jonas feels his throat constrict and he gasps for air.

Anamika takes his hand and looks into his eyes. "It's okay, Jonas. It's just you. Don't be afraid."

He takes a sip of water. Shuts his eyes. Squeezes Anamika's hand.

"Let's just breathe together. Find your breath in your belly and take it up into your lungs. Breathe in 'here.' Breathe out 'now.'"

Jonas turns his attention to here and now and breathes in and out. His breath slows, throat opens, and he becomes an open channel once again.

"Thanks for that," Jonas gently removes his hand from hers. "I do that myself sometimes, if I'm having difficulty meditating or something: breathe in 'here' and breathe out 'now.' I thought I invented it. I thought it was personal."

Anamika smiles softly. "Yes, it *is* personal. And it's something we share, I guess. I think we'll find that there's a lot of very personal things we have in common."

They sit quietly for a while and smoke another cigarette. Anamika orders more chai.

"I guess I must have tuned into you when I did that dream exercise about interpreting my life like a book. Right? That literary-life-interpretation idea became important to me. It was like an extension of what D says about everything being symbolic or metaphorical. He calls it all a dream or a play. But I like the literary analysis thing; it's more, well, personal for me."

"Right. You connected with me in your dream, tuned into my frequency. It doesn't matter that your dream exercise didn't occur at the same time that I was actually giving a very similar exercise in satsang. Doesn't matter if it was a bit different, more tailored to your personality. It was there and you tapped into it. There must have been something in that exercise that you wanted to do!"

"And the poems. What about them? They rocked my world. They and the voice—well, you I guess—freed me up so I could come here. Otherwise, I'd never have taken the risk and come with Bruce to India. I would have been too afraid of such a change. I'm not like Bruce, not adventurous. But after that weird stuff happened, I was open to anything. If *that* was possible, anything was possible, you know? The world became a different place. It, like, opened up."

"I'd love to read the poems sometime! Poems come through me sometimes too. And words do too, quite often. I don't know what I can tell you. You weren't tapping in to me, I don't think, unless it was in a dream state. A poem could come from anywhere, anybody, any part of you. Or it could arise from the confluence of your other lives, like a mountain rising up when tectonic plates shift and converge. A poem, too, can be an event, a collision of forces, sometimes literally earth-shattering, and a thing in itself, a beautiful thing in the world that others can see and enjoy, climb to the top of, or read from start to finish. And be inspired by to create something themselves.

"It's a mysterious process, creativity. Making stuff out of nothing. Isn't it? We are all creative artists making our lives and collaborating with others. 'Co-creating' is the buzzword in new age-y circles, though I like to avoid the term because it's been so freely tossed around that its meaning is emptying out, like spring water falling from the mouth of a gourd."

As Anamika talks, visions arise within Jonas: of the Himalayan mountains forming through aggressive, almost violent, creative convergences; of Shiva dancing the destruction of the world while the seeds of creation burst open at his feet. Of a circle of small, nearly naked dark-skinned children standing on dry, cracked earth, singing a chant-like song in musical, rhythmic voices, occasionally erupting in tinkling laughter. Jonas feels like he is actually there, is one of the children in the circle.

She catches the big yellow gourd in her small, supple hands, red-and-orange woven bracelets swinging from her wrists, and takes a sip from it of the sweet water. Swaying her narrow hips, she sings the song that will bring the rain, and the rest join in. *Imvula, imvula, chapha-chapha-chapha.* When the song reaches a crescendo, she throws the gourd to another child in the circle, as upright as she can in order to keep the water in the vessel. Just a little of the precious water sprays out of the gourd as it flies through the air. She laughs happily as her big sister catches it and drinks, wipes her mouth with the back of her hand and smiles, and begins the song again. *Imvula, imvula, chapha-chapha-chapha.* She looks up at the sky expectantly.

"Anamika," Jonas brings himself back to the restaurant table. He takes a long sip of water. He doesn't quite know how to ask this, but feels he has to. "Did you know that I was here?"

Anamika looks at Jonas through the steam of her new cup of chai, and squints a little.

"Nope. That was a surprise. But I'm sure happy you're here too."

∾

Anamika and Jonas spend the day together, bopping about on her scooter. They have fun in the "foreigners" supermarket, which seems to have everything a spiritual tourist could want—from yoga mats and essential oils to real cheese (a rarity, and something that Anamika has been missing lately)—and it's air-conditioned. A Westerner's oasis. Jonas buys smokes and groceries for him and Bruce, and Anamika picks up some toiletries and cheese. They try to find the store where Bruce and Jonas bought beer, but Jonas can't recall where the rickshaw driver took them—somewhere deep in the dusty maze of streets in crowded downtown Tiruvannamalai, where Indians sell their wares to each other—away from Ramana's ashram and the nearby shops, restaurants, and satsang venues that cater to tourists and spiritual seekers. So they just drive around for a while.

On the way home, they stop at Ramana's ashram and poke around in the bookstore there. Jonas buys a white canvas shoulder bag that every other foreigner seems to have, with a red line drawing of Mt. Arunachala on it and the words, "Arunachala, thou dost root out the ego of those who meditate on thee in the heart, oh Arunachala."

Anamika likes having Jonas close to her. She's curious about their relationship. There's lots going on there. Almost too much. Yet at the same time, it's so very comfortable. Like home. There's a tension between these opposed feelings of complexity and comfort. At times during their day together, an unusual image appears before her eyes of two warm, glowing spherical balls of light hovering close to each other, then moving this way and that, like images in a cheesy sci-fi flick, but always ending up near each other, electric currents occasionally passing between them.

And, yes, Anamika did quite like the kiss at her door last night. That's crossed her mind more than once today. Especially how Jonas brushed her hair back. The intimacy of it. And she sees the way he looks at her when he thinks she's not looking. She can read him like a book. A good, interesting book. One that's been on her reading list for a while.

When they get back to Anamika's place in the late afternoon, they find a note under the door. It's from Bruce. He'd gone to Amma's morning darshan and was hoping to see Anamika today, since she wasn't giving satsang and he knew it wasn't one of her days at Ramu's.

After she reads the note aloud, Anamika glances at Jonas who looks at his feet. She knows what's going on.

"Let me drive you home, and I'll see if Bruce is there. Maybe hang with him for a little while. And you too of course, if you're up for it. Unless Bruce wants it to be just him and me. You know. Is that okay?"

When they arrive, Bruce is napping in his white boxer shorts, lying on his back, his muscular limbs loosely sprawled across the bed, golden hairs covering every tanned inch of him. Even in his sleep he inhabits his body gracefully. He looks peaceful. Strong. And excruciatingly beautiful. A sun god at rest. Oh my. Anamika swallows. Bruce opens his eyes.

"Hey you!" A sleepy smile stretches his mouth open, and he extends his hand to Anamika, ready to pull her down beside him. "How did you get in?"

"I'm here too," Jonas says quickly from across the room, busy with something on purpose.

Bruce sits up and swings his feet to the floor. "Oh, hi man. Didn't see you there." He puts his elbows on his knees and runs his hands through his wavy blond hair. Clears his throat. "So, what have you guys been up to?"

"Jonas and I went for breakfast together and then drove around for a while on my scooter."

"Right. I guess you two have a lot to talk about, eh."

Anamika looks over at Jonas, but he's quietly unpacking groceries with his back toward them, obviously trying to give them some space. "Yeah. I get the feeling we've only scratched the surface."

"Right," says Bruce.

"Hey," Jonas turns toward them. "I just remembered. I wanted to Skype my dad today. So I'm going to Ramu's to use the computer. Maybe I'll catch you guys later."

Anamika smiles to herself. These are two kind, thoughtful guys who obviously value their friendship. Bruce looks embarrassed as he nods goodbye to Jonas. Anamika gives Jonas a little hug.

After he's gone, Bruce pats the place next to where he's sitting on the bed. Anamika sits beside him, but a little farther away.

"So how was Amma today?" Anamika asks.

"Great as usual, thanks," Bruce responds rather formally, Anamika thinks. Something passes over his face. "I like having both of you amazing women in my life!" He winks at her. "No disrespect intended."

"None taken." Anamika waits for more.

"Really, though. I feel you each give me something important. Amma lets me be silent and sends me into bliss. And you, dear Anamikaji. You take me to different places. I'm talking satsang, of course." Bruce's eyes dance with mischief. "You send me into bliss too. A different kind of bliss. Know what I mean?"

"No, Bruce. What do you mean?" Anamika's tone is mock-serious, but her eyes aren't mocking at all.

Bruce leans through the distance between them and takes her into his arms. "Anamika. What's going on," he breathes into her hair.

They just hold each other for a while until Anamika disentangles herself.

"I don't know." She looks up at the ceiling fan, its blades spinning so fast they are a blur. "Jonas and I need to explore what we are to each other."

"I know," Bruce whispers. He cups Anamika's face in both of his large hands and studies it as if he's trying to commit it to memory. He scans her entire face, from her high forehead to her little chin, up and across her prominent cheekbones, over her dark eyes and all the way up to the brown hair parted on her head. "I love you," he says to the top of her head.

Anamika lets herself be drawn into his kiss, his arms, his body.

The sun sets quickly here. It's dark when they finish making love. Anamika gets into her salwar kameez as fast as she can, suddenly worried that Jonas will return. Bruce obviously doesn't want her to leave yet and invites her to stay for dinner, but she needs to go. They'll see each other at satsang tomorrow evening. She wants the rest of tomorrow to herself.

Anamika is feeling confused, discombobulated, as she gets on her scooter and drives home, craving the solitude of her own place. She needs to be by herself. Things are spinning so fast they are a blur.

Man oh man. Maybe she doesn't know everything after all.

~

Jonas hasn't spoken to his dad since coming to India. And he hadn't thought of Skyping him until he mentioned it to Bruce and Anamika. He just needed a plausible excuse to get out of there. It's 4:30 in the afternoon, 4:00 in the morning in Vancouver. His dad won't be up for work for another hour or so. He's in his dad's future.

He walks to the paratha stand to kill some time, and orders paratha and a Coke. What a day. He closes his eyes and turns inward. He sees D's light-filled eyes and wants to keep himself there, with D, with no thought, in peace and tranquility, away from the so-called world. The world of mirrors. D says that the more one keeps turned inward, silent and still, the more frequent the taste of the eternal bliss—until it begins to take over and the transient world recedes until it dissolves completely.

But D would probably tell him that he's running away from stuff right now. And you can't get "there" by running away.

So, D, what do you have to say about Anamika's teachings? Especially all those partner selves and incarnations everywhere? His and Anamika's undeniable connection? Huh? Jonas waits patiently for an answer. Just thinking about the multiplicity of selves and dimensions exhausts him at this moment. Or maybe he's just tired because his hangover is back. Alternate realities. Many worlds. Universes. It reminds him of what he's read in quantum physics about the multiverse—the popular rendering of it anyway. And science fiction. Problem is, he doesn't think it's fiction at all. Or at least no more so than anything else.

His paratha comes, and he rips the slightly sweet, flaky, layered disc of bread into little bits and pours the small bowl of curry that comes with it over the heap of shredded paratha. He tunes his mental activity down to low, keeping to only the present moment, staying with D. He glorifies in the messiness on his fingers as he eats with them, using them like tongs.

Story, Jonas. It's just another story. Phenomena. It doesn't matter if it's appearing in the world you see, or on your inner HD TV, or another life in a different time period, or this one here, or all of them altogether. It's all fantasy, an illusion created by ego. And its role is to help you see what you need to, to burn away the armor built by conditioning and set you free. None of it has to do with what is really true, what is eternal. And there is no need for the story to be complex. There are only a few issues needing attention, and these keep cycling through, over and over. In one life or many lives, it's all the same.

That's what he thinks he hears D saying to him. Or what he thinks he would say. Jonas doesn't know how much of it comes from his own imagination and memory. Probably all of it. He feels vaguely dissatisfied with the response, in any case.

Jonas walks to Ramu's and gets on a computer.

"Jonas? Is that you?" The image of his dad, sleepy-eyed, fills the screen. He looks old, vulnerable. Jonas is taken aback. When was the last time he saw him? A few months ago? Maybe six? He usually found a good excuse not to see his father. He just didn't want to hear more criticism of his life since he left academia behind. Working at a print shop didn't live up to his father's expectations of him, he was pretty sure.

"How are you? How is India? God, it's good to see you. You look good. Healthy. I've missed you." His dad's smile is warm and genuine. He has deeper creases around his mouth and grey stubble on his jaw.

"Hi Dad!" Jonas is surprised to feel such excitement seeing his father. They talk together for a good ten minutes before his father has to go and get ready for work. Jonas tells him about the magnet mountain and a little about D and the retreat. He doesn't mention Anamika.

"You take care, son. I love you."

Are those actual tears in his father's eyes? "I love you too."

Afterward, Jonas can't take the smile off his face. He feels elated. He goes outside and smokes a cigarette, relishing in his feeling, the connection he felt with his father.

He can't remember the last time his dad said he loved him. Has his father changed? Or is it he himself who's changed? When was the last time he told his dad he loved him? And he does. He seemed so...meek. Not the brusque and assertive man of business he knew. Or thought he knew.

At this point, Jonas doesn't know if he ever really knew anything at all.

CHAPTER 26

Anamika sleeps until late morning, and lies in bed lazily recalling her dreams, the sense of them and the stories. When she arises, she moves slowly. It's already quite hot in her little place. She showers and eats a leisurely breakfast. It's good to be by herself. She's just finished her boiled egg and chapati when she hears a knock on her door. She opens it and finds Maryam, one of the "original five" to come to her satsang. She is a petite woman in her early twenties, and today she looks just like a little girl. A lost little girl who has been crying: her large dark eyes are bloodshot and rimmed in pink. Anamika welcomes her in and offers her some freshly brewed tea. Maryam accepts the cup in trembling hands.

"I'm sorry, Anamikaji. I didn't know if I should come, but I, I didn't know... where else should I go." She barely gets the last few words out of her mouth. Tears roll down her face.

"Maryam, I'm happy you came to see me." Anamika takes her hand. "What's going on right now?"

"My brother. He was not a good brother to me. I have only just remembered. Growing up in Tehran, we had to share a bedroom. Last night, the images come to me. Horrible pictures in my mind. I have only just remembered now. It's too much for me to bear." Maryam covers her face in her hands and sobs. Anamika gently rests her hand on her back. She waits until Maryam finishes crying and offers her a tissue.

"I'm very sorry to bother you like this," she says as she dabs at her eyes with the tissue. "It's just...I am in so much pain." Maryam's breath turns choppy and shallow, and she begins to hiccup.

"Maryam, look at me, please. See me. I am here. We are here together. That's all. It's just us."

Maryam smiles slightly through some fresh tears. "But he is here, too. I feel him inside of me!" Her face suddenly contorts and she lets out a loud wail. "What do I do?"

Anamika needs a moment. She hasn't dealt with this kind of thing before. She's not sure what Maryam needs and if she can even give it. Who is she to help anyone anyway?

She gives Maryam a hug, and holds her tightly for a while until this wave of anguish leaves her body. But it feels like the waves of her pain aren't going to subside, and will fill the room and drown them both. What to do?

When Maryam goes to the toilet, Anamika stands very still in the middle of the room. She opens her inner senses wide, and formulates a question: How can I help?

Maryam returns. Wordlessly, through gesture only, Anamika has Maryam stand and face her. Anamika rubs her own arm from wrist to shoulder, up and down, and then brings her hand up to her face. She brings her other hand to her face and gives it a gentle massage—forehead, eyebrows, temples, cheekbones, lips, taking special care at the point where the lower and upper jaw bones meet. She has her eyes closed. When she finishes massaging her face, she opens her eyes. Maryam is massaging her own face, too.

Anamika's arms hang loosely at her sides. She waits for Maryam to finish her face massage, and just looks into her eyes for a while. Maryam takes a long, shaky breath, exhales. Anamika takes a long breath, exhales. Maryam takes a full, deep breath. Anamika follows suit. Maryam moves her head from side to side on her neck, stretching it this way and that. Anamika does the same. Maryam sighs noisily, and so does Anamika. Anamika moves her arms over her head and stretches. And so does Maryam. Together, they stretch their bodies and breathe.

And soon their movement becomes more free-flowing. Maryam makes shapes in the air with her arms and hands. Anamika is struck by their fluid beauty. They remind her of the mudras she's seen in images of Indian goddesses. She follows her gestures, but in her own way, and lifts a straight leg, balletically, behind her. She feels the air molecules shifting around her.

Anamika and Maryam are moving together in a dance, changing shapes, flowing effortlessly, freely, sometimes adapting their movements to the other's, open to change, to possibility. Maryam is now twirling and smiling, her dark eyes shining as tears stream down her cheeks and into the river of their dancing.

When their dance is over, Maryam embraces Anamika and thanks her, kisses her lightly on her cheek, and leaves. Anamika can feel the vibrations lingering in the room, and she lies flat on the floor, arms outstretched and legs in a "V." Her body sinks into the hard floor as if it's sinking into a soft and fragrant bath. She feels deeply calm. And she drifts off somewhere, perfectly content.

"One of the things I like about being here at the foot of this magic mountain is that everyone who comes here is pulled in some way. It's not really a physically beautiful place, and aside from the one major Shiva temple in town, there's not much here of cultural, historical significance. But there's this mountain, Arunachala, as ordinary looking as it is. And there's Ramana Maharshi's legacy. And people come here from all over the world to ask questions, to find what's really true, to take a good look inside." Anamika pauses in satsang, and remains quiet for a minute. She notices that some have their eyes closed. There is a calm settling in. Anamika continues to speak slowly and quietly.

"Of course, this can be a difficult journey. That's part of the deal when you go inside and look around. And here, we've not only let most of our daily distractions go, but we're also in a place of power, where the physical world is almost transparent. One could say that the veil of maya, illusion, is thin here at this mountain. So we've got the environment supporting us, too. The stage is set. And, for many, a different kind of drama unfolds. An interior drama. Stuff comes up from the deep past, or difficult challenges are presented.

"I know about this, believe me. I'm not immune. I might have different resources for dealing with stuff, maybe even extra resources, but it doesn't mean that it's always easy or that I know what to do all the time or that I'm always happy." The room is very quiet, as if everyone is holding their breath. Or as if she's the only person there. It's just her. But she continues to talk as if there are other separate beings listening.

"I know that each of you already feels compassion for others. Tolerance, acceptance, kindness. You wouldn't be here in this place if you didn't. And really, what beautiful people are here! No wonder so many don't want to leave, and so many return. It's a kind of utopia. Everyone is so cool, and everyone shares a purpose. But shit comes up, doesn't it. Doesn't matter where you are. There you are.

"And we can be hard on ourselves if that happens, right? I mean, here we are, in the most spiritually supportive place on earth, and we're depressed or angry or bitter or hurt or confused or trapped within our past. How embarrassing! We should be peaceful and happy here, and always *always* present!" The silence is broken by scattered laughter. Some heads nod in agreement. She's struck a chord.

"And yet. Something about being here brings it all up, doesn't it. So, what I'd like to do today is to turn that compassion you feel for others onto yourself. You've been through a lot. You're going through a lot.

"If your eyes are closed, keep them closed. If not, close them if you like. Feel the beautiful calm in the room right now." A few moments pass.

"Okay. Now feel what's inside of you right now. Is there a place where something uncomfortable or painful is living? Has something recently come up? If so, find it now. Look at it if you can, see the images or sounds attached to it. Don't relive the experience. Just observe it as it exists inside of you right now. Keep breathing. Let's stay with the observation for a few minutes.

"Now, if you're ready, feel into it. Feel past whatever anger for someone else may be there—past whatever may have been done to you—and into the hurt." Anamika keeps a careful watch over the group, ready to respond if it looks like someone needs her. Like Maryam did that morning. "Just feel it. Feel it *gently*.

"And now, I'd like you to let it know that it's welcome here. This pain is a child, a hurt child, you as a child. Let your compassion enfold it." A few people in the room seem to be crying softly. Kris and Gabi are holding hands. Maryam is hugging herself. "This is nothing but a beautiful thing. You aren't prodding at a wound, you are looking at it and acknowledging it. Bathe it in warm, healing water. Bathe it in your compassion.

"Now I'd like you to put your palms together at the center of your chest, as if you were saying Namaste, as if you were praying. If you like, bow your head a bit. And let's just sit like this for a while."

Anamika places her palms together in the prayerful posture, and immediately feels centered, grounded. She breathes deeply, and feels the room settle back into calm. She notices the color of the auras change around the people who were crying. She sees some bent heads and is inexplicably moved.

"Feel the respect you have for yourself. Everything you do, everything that you've done, has been good enough." She lets that sink in for a couple of minutes and notices the energy change subtly again.

"And finally, feel the unconditional love you have for yourself, and especially for that little child inside of you. So sweet, so vulnerable. She did nothing wrong. She just got hurt."

~

After the self-compassion meditation, the group takes a ten-minute break. It's very quiet; only a few people speak to each other in low tones. When they gather again, Anamika says that she doesn't have something in particular to talk about, so the floor is open to questions about anything.

Bruce's hand flies up. "Anamikaji, can you talk about what happens when you dream?"

Anamika smiles and closes her eyes. "Yes, of course." Anamika formulates her next words carefully.

"I know that Ramana has a different approach to this, and I see the truth in his teachings. But again, I can only tell you what I myself know. I don't mean to argue with the great sage; I only provide another perspective." She opens her eyes and looks at the group. Their faces are open and receptive. Bruce nods, understanding. Anamika lets her words fall out freely now.

"I'd like to talk about two main things that go on when you sleep and dream: first, the effect on the body. Of course, everyone knows that sleep, rest, is restorative for the body. But so are dreams. Dreams affect your body in the same way that your thoughts and beliefs do—because your body is a living expression of who you are at each moment. Scientific research has shown that the brain-body can't distinguish between imagination and 'reality.' Imagination and emotion have chemical, hormonal, and neurological equivalents. There is a direct relationship. Imagining some event fully produces the same chemicals in the body that the actual experience of that event does. Same with dreams. Your body goes through changes when you sleep, and the activity in dreams causes those changes.

"There is much healing that happens here, on subtle levels that your conscious mind is unaware of. You think that to avoid cancer, say, you must do this and that, don't smoke, eat organically, live a clean life. But you don't take into account what goes on in dreams—and you're asleep for about one-third of your life! Again, the physical does not have a separate, independent reality; it's a symbolic and fluid representation. You think you can exert control over your body by using other physical means. But the living body is constantly being shaped by you on very deep levels that you rarely access consciously. And your dream life is one of these arenas. You make your body, change your body's make-up, in your dreams as surely as you do in waking life. There are choices you make in dreams, too, for various reasons important to your growth. These affect you on all levels, as everything does. So, dreams help you physically heal yourself and find answers to questions that appear in the body.

"And the second main thing that goes on is this: dreams also provide a fertile ground for making creative choices that move you in different directions in your lives, into new areas of growth and exploration. One way they do this is they give you a place where you can interact with not only your partner selves, but also with others more separate but equally important to you. There is much trading of knowledge that occurs and the solving of problems together. Emotions are expressed and released, too—emotions that you might have buried in waking life—and their expression clears the way for change and new growth.

"Another way dreams help nudge you in different directions: the less structured environment in dreams allows you to try on new things, experiment with possibilities and potentials of being. It is like a playground. You can be and do in dreams in ways unimaginable in waking perception. Time and space don't exist, gravity doesn't exist, that is, the so-called rules of the physical world don't apply; there are no restrictions but the ones you impose on yourself. So, you not only recreate your body in dreams but also your very self, and you can create in a freer way than you do—or you *think* you do—in the physical world."

Anamika stops talking, having answered Bruce's question as fully as she can. But moments later, she realizes there's one more important issue needing to be addressed.

"And finally, on a different note: people talk about the symbolism in dreams, and much is made of dream interpretation and working with reappearing symbols. Psychoanalysis is built around that, right? Freud. You know what I'm talking about. It's always amazed me that this approach to dreams seems obvious to everyone. It's pretty much the conventional approach. The popular one, anyway. People look in dream-symbol books and online to "find out" what their dreams *mean*. They take for granted that there is some hidden meaning or message there for them in their dreams.

"But no book about dream symbolism will really help you understand your dreams. You don't need to look outside of yourself. Only you know the meaning of your dreams—it's your own dream, after all. Personal. And you only need ask yourself a few questions to get the most meaning from your dream. Like, for example, 'So, what does a tunnel mean to me? When did I last go through a tunnel? What kind of tunnel was it? How did it feel to me?' We each have a personal symbology. And sometimes drawing the dream images and writing about them will allow their meaning to come forth.

"But what is the most amazing to me is that while everyone is interested in what such-and-such a symbol in a dream means, no one takes that approach to physical life! Waking life. 'Reality.' *It's all symbolic*, of course. Everything you perceive anywhere, in dreams and around you right now—symbols. All symbols. If you want to understand yourself and your world, interpret these. Just as you would a dream.

"Okay," Anamika says with a smile. "Now I'm done."

Priya has her hand up, and Anamika nods to her. "Anamikaji, who is it who is in the dream? Many times I dream of my grandmother. She has died. I miss her very much. I feel happy when I wake up if I am seeing her in my dream. Is it really her I am seeing like this? Oh, I hope you say yes!"

Anamika laughs at this, along with several others. "Yes, Priya! But…"

"Oh, no. I think I must be leaving now," Priya quips.

"My mother died recently, Priya. And I often dream of her. I dream of who she was *to me*. That's how she existed in my life, and in my dreams the relationship still exists. So, yes, she is the woman in my dream that she was, but who she was is my creation, in an important way. We've discussed this before, yes?"

"Yes, but sometimes it is hard to keep remembering like this. I understand it here," Priya touches her chest. "But not always here," she says, tapping her head.

"Yup, I get it. However, just to confuse matters: I also communicate with my mother's greater Self, who is and isn't the mother I knew. And that occurs both when I dream and when I'm awake. And here's another thing, and I hope it doesn't confuse you even more! Your grandmother is always her greater Self too, and in that way, you do connect with her, though it might not be with the personality that you're familiar with. She might look like your grandmother when you recall the dream from a waking perspective, but in the dream—and remember, dreams aren't physical—she doesn't really have an appearance, or not one you could see with your eyes, anyway. But it's still her, in the fullest sense; you can feel her. It's the whole crystal, not just one face, not just the side that you've been used to seeing the light refract through.

"In dreams we connect with who is important to us—the greater Selves of who we know in waking reality (including our beloved pets!), our partner selves, and others. And some of us get around! It depends on the greater Self. Some enjoy large and complex constellations; others prefer them small and simple. But, like in waking reality, it's really all about us."

Jonas has his hand up. "That all sounds good. If a bit complicated. But, Anamika, what about love? Where is love in all this?"

Anamika swallows. She looks at Jonas and something passes between them. For a moment she feels as if she's looking out of Jonas's eyes at herself, sitting on a chair in front of everyone. She looks so small. Fleeting disorientation. Then she's back in her chair looking at Jonas sitting cross-legged on the floor. It seems to her that she's never seen anyone look so serious.

"Where is love in all this? It's the reason for it all. It's what brings your lives into relationship with other lives. It's the light that shines through the crystal of your whole Self. It's what holds your constellation together. It's the confluence of bodies and beings, selves and cells. Love is where the tide meets the river. Love is the song that sings itself. It is the air you breathe."

V: PATHS

(Air)

We shall not cease from exploration
And the end of all our exploring
Will be to arrive where we started
And know the place for the first time.

— *T. S. Eliot, from "Little Gidding"*

CHAPTER 27

"Love is in the air!" Bruce sings as he and Jonas wait for Anamika to emerge from inside Ramu's Travel. "Doo-doo-doo, doo-doo-doo…" Jonas is feeling especially thoughtful tonight after Anamika's satsang. How can Bruce be so light-hearted all the time? Maybe he's enlightened, he thinks whimsically. Then again, maybe he really is! Things do come easily to his handsome pal Bruce. Wouldn't that be a kicker.

Jonas is getting caught in his mind, in "the story," as D would say. He has an overwhelming desire that is making him identify with his "I" that doesn't really exist, and that "I-dentification" is keeping him separate, keeping him from receiving the grace he had been offered so freely on retreat, those openings into enlightenment. He has been caught up in this since he met Anamika. What is that desire? The desire for truth. Capital "T" Truth. Jonas doesn't feel what D calls "the hunger for freedom." He doesn't have that great need to surrender it all that Brahma expressed on retreat. He first wants the Truth. He hungers for Truth.

Is it true that freedom from the illusory, transitory world is the be-all-and-end-all? Is enlightenment the final and noblest achievement and what we should all be shooting for? For the sake of ourselves and "the world"? Are we here to find our way back home, to God, who, as D once said, has been calling to us over lifetimes? Or rather is it true what Anamika speaks of? Rather than walking through the doorway that is D and falling into the bliss of the eternal Self, should Jonas be open to his other selves and learn and grow with them, fulfilling potentials, discovering possibilities, playing? Does he create his own reality? D would say it is created, but not by him, and that it's all orchestrated to lead him to his freedom. And the character's "reality" is only for burning away. Until there is only what's true left. What's really real. The true reality.

Jonas doesn't doubt the illusory nature of time, space, and physical reality. He doesn't doubt the reflective, metaphorical nature of what he sees around him, his life—call it dream, story, novel, play, movie. He doesn't doubt the necessity to go inside to see what's really going on. Both Anamika and D share this common ground. He stands with them there.

Here is where Jonas struggles: If he does create his reality through his deeply ingrained beliefs, as Anamika says, is he also *creating this idea of enlightenment*? For that matter, if Anamika's teachings are true, are all of the great masters, spiritual teachers, and Indian yogis that he's read about (and he includes Jesus among the great masters)—those who are enlightened and who can seemingly perform miracles, like being in two places at once, like not needing to breathe or eat, like creating something out of nothing, as well as those who are simply awake and embody love, like D—are they all creating their realities through their beliefs too? Jonas doesn't doubt the miracles; he's experienced some himself. But are they *enlightened* because they believe in it?

Were Jonas's experiences with D solely due to the creative power of Jonas's own belief? His belief in D? Moreover, is D himself enlightened because he believes *he is?*

D's words don't come from him. He's said that himself. And the fluidity with which they fall out of D's mouth reminds Jonas a little of his own automatic writing, the writing that doesn't come from him. So too does D's body get animated when he's speaking to someone in satsang—in a way similar to famous channelers Jonas has seen on YouTube. Maybe D is simply channeling Ramana Maharshi! Or channeling his own greater Self, the larger entity Anamika speaks of, the sum of all of his incarnations. The multi-faced crystal turning in the air.

Another kind of big "S" self. The kind that exists *within* dimensions of existence, not *as* the nature of existence itself.

All of this is what makes Jonas thoughtful. And anxious. How can he know for sure what is true? Isn't this why he's here in India? Why he's alive, period? It seems that Jonas has come to a fork in the road. There are two paths now. Which one does he walk down? Each path has practical consequences. Jonas thinks it through logically.

Path One: If it's true that everyone creates his reality like an artist, including the gurus and masters, then one needs to open oneself to how one is doing it and why. Learning, exploring, and growing—these are what one does on this path. One *does* something. The locus of action and control is in you, the fuller you. It's all about you—you as your individual self and you in conjunction with your greater, multidimensional Self and partner selves or incarnations. The existence of God, or whatever name you want to use, Love, All That Is, Consciousness, is of little consequence on this path, he thinks. He's not sure about that though—hence his question to Anamika. He's not sure where this path "ends" either. If it does.

Path Two: But if it's true that you aren't really in control of anything—in fact, there's really no "you" at all—all one needs to do is surrender, relax, let it all unfold as it will anyway, being divinely orchestrated and all. You just receive what's given; you get out of your own way. If you get caught up in "doing" stuff that you identify with, then you get caught up in the dream, the story, and you remain in the illusory world of subject and object, on the rollercoaster ride of joy and pain, desire and fear. So you don't "do" anything except meditate and feel the aliveness of your existence, your heart. Be still and silent, and dissociate from the world and activity; and when stuff comes up, you let it burn. And thus the illusion dissolves along with the habits of mind that keep you in your hypnotic trance and maintain the separate "I" character—and your true nature is revealed, which is unchanging, which is Self, God, that shining ocean of love. And that's where the path ends. It's all about not-you.

To do or not to do? *That* is the question. And of course, the age-old "free will vs. destiny" dilemma is tied up in this, too. Path One: You do, you create, you have free will. Path Two: You cease doing, you surrender, you let destiny do its thing without you. Most world religions and twelve-step recovery programs take Path Two: God is in control. Let go, let God. Most "new age" philosophies take Path One: You are in control. It's your world, make it good, be the change.

"Enlightenment"—now Jonas knows what it is. Problem is, he doesn't know if belief in it is required to achieve it. And if belief is a prerequisite, then it's not the ultimate Truth. Anamika wins. But…but what if D is pointing toward something *beyond* Anamika's worlds? That is, what if Anamika's "deeply ingrained beliefs" and D's "conditioning" are *the same thing*? Both beliefs and conditioning engender individual realities, which are really fictional. Can you transcend your beliefs and hence personal reality like you can burn away your conditioning, your karma, those recurring issues? If so, one could just step out of the matrix of conditioning, beliefs, and personally created reality, whether multidimensional or in-your-face. If this is the case, the be-all-and-end-all is indeed beyond duality—beyond anything "in particular," as D would say—and waking up from the dream, Jonas's dream, Anamika's dream, is where the ultimate Truth lives.

He has a sneaking suspicion the bigger problem is that no matter how hard he tries to think this two-path thing through, he's not going to get anywhere. Is he positing yet another philosophical duality, a Taoist yin-yang circle that should be sent spinning until its two halves blur together into one? It's probably another one of those problems where a solution just can't be arrived at intellectually. Both D and Anamika would likely agree on that one, too.

Anamika walks out of Ramu's, and when Jonas sees her again, he feels his mental knots loosen and fall apart. The two paths dissolve for now. It's just her. Just Anamika—sweet, beautiful, *familiar* Anamika. He breathes relief, and his shoulders relax. Why so serious, anyway.

But then there's Bruce: Bruce playfully grabbing Anamika's hand in one of his and circling the other one around her waist. As he dances with her in the dusty road outside Ramu's, he belts out in a loud sing-song baritone, "Love is in the air, doo-doo-doo, doo-doo-doo, love is in the air!" Anamika is laughing. The ends of her long blue-green dupatta-scarf do their own floaty dance around her back, and her hair joins in.

CHAPTER 28

The egg biryani at the Holy Mountain restaurant in Tiru is delicious, and comes with a whole boiled egg sitting in a little pool of sauce on top of a hill of rice and veggies. Eggs are the most satisfying and familiar protein Jonas can find in restaurants in this holy-veg town, and he eats a lot of them. Even though he figures his body has adjusted to the "pure veg" diet here, he often craves meat, lots of it. He dreams of sizzling bacon next to his eggs, fat juicy hamburgers, a tender sirloin steak smoking on the grill. He should ask Anamika if they can arrange to get some contraband chicken at her friends' restaurant soon. Just the thought of biting into a piece of tasty, moist chicken flesh makes his mouth water. Jonas is sure his already thin frame has gotten even thinner. He mixes the sauce up with the rice and veggies, leaving some rice plain for variety's sake, and takes a bite out of the egg.

It was Anamika's idea to come into town for a late dinner after her satsang. Jonas hesitated; his money is almost all gone, and even though rooming with Bruce costs him next to nothing, he has to be thrifty to make sure his money lasts until his departure date—which is coming up soon, though Jonas prefers not to think about it. Restaurants in town are more expensive than the ones in their neighborhood (dinner costs a whole three or four Canadian dollars instead of a buck or so), and then there's the cost of the rickshaw. Three on a scooter is nothing for Indians—Jonas has seen a family of five on one motorbike—but if the three include big, brawny Bruce, it would be pretty uncomfortable.

Anamika responded to Jonas's hesitation by taking both of his large hands in her little ones, and looking into his eyes had said, *Jonas.* (And oh, he likes how she says his name, likes it as much as how D says it, but in a different way.) *Jonas, I have money now, more than I need, and it would make me very happy if I could share it with you.* She then opened up her cloth shoulder bag and showed him all the loose rupee bills inside. *Look at what people gave me just for tonight's satsang!* The dinner and rickshaw were on her.

Holy Mountain is a large, spacious restaurant popular with tourists, and has outdoor and indoor sections and an adjoining store that sells loose, colorful clothing, mala beads, and books about many different Indian gurus. When Jonas, Anamika, and Bruce walk in, Jonas notices *The Autobiography of a Yogi* in the display window and gives Bruce a little nudge.

Bruce acts very cozy with Anamika—seating himself next to her at their table, then sliding very close to her on the bench seat and touching her in a familiar-casual way during conversation. Jonas notices he doesn't do anything that would suggest romantic possessiveness however, like holding hands. They'd make an attractive couple, Jonas acknowledges painfully: the delicate, dark, ethereally beautiful woman and the athletic, blond, ridiculously good-looking man. Yin and yang; feminine and masculine personified.

They have finished dinner and are waiting for their dessert: kulfi, which is really ice cream—ice cream! another protein Jonas is happy about, and Indians know how to make it—when a dark-skinned middle-aged Indian man who's been staring at Anamika during dinner approaches their table. This isn't unusual. Often when Anamika is out, people approach her; she's a public figure here in Satsang Central. But this man isn't smiling.

"You are against our Hindu religion. You should go home. You are not welcome here." He stands close to where Anamika sits, towering over her, his nostrils flaring wide and his thick black moustache twitching with pent-up anger.

Anamika gazes up at him silently. Jonas recognizes him as the man who noisily got up and left that first satsang he'd attended of hers, the one about karma. Bruce immediately leaps to his feet, stands tall, and says authoritatively, "Excuse me, sir, but we're just having a quiet dinner here."

"Perhaps we can speak together another time," Anamika adds softly. Jonas sits and watches, feeling another knot form, in his belly this time.

Bruce throws his shoulders back and takes a step closer to the man, who glares at Anamika and waves his finger in her face. "I am telling you. No more of this speaking against the Hindu religion. You know nothing about karma! Go home," he growls and then turns abruptly and walks away. Bruce sits back down heavily.

"Are you okay?" Jonas asks Anamika. "That was pretty intense, eh."

Anamika looks a little shaken. Bruce gives her a one-arm hug from his seat beside her.

"Thanks, guys. I guess I'm okay. I've got to cook this one through, I think. Later." When their kulfi arrives, they eat in silence.

Once they are all on the street outside the Holy Mountain and looking for a rickshaw, Bruce clears his throat. "Uh, Anamika. Speaking of going home. Um. Jonas and I have return tickets and leave in less than a couple of weeks. That's the plan, anyway. What about you? Any plans?"

"Wow. So soon?" Anamika turns her head toward Jonas and catches his eye. There's a crease between her eyebrows. He thinks he sees a question mark there too, especially for him. They have barely begun to get to know each other. And he's been waiting for her his whole life, it seems. At least.

"Yeah, I know," Bruce's voice is low and serious.

"I have an open ticket, myself. And a six-month visa that's renewable. It's probably up pretty soon, though. I better check when I get home. Thanks for reminding me."

On the ride back in the rickshaw, with the three of them squeezed close together in the little seat behind the driver, Jonas's stomach hurts. That knot hasn't gone away. He begins to feel nauseous. There's stuff inside that's going to come up one way or another. So he decides to just say what he needs to. Let it out. Something about driving through the dark along the dusty, bumpy roads makes it easier. As soon as he begins to talk, the nausea dissipates.

"Look, Anamika, Bruce. I think there's something we all need to talk about." Jonas notices that Bruce is holding Anamika's hand against her thigh in the squishy dark of the rickshaw seat. "Well, I do, anyway." He makes himself keep talking. "Of course, I don't know what's going on with the two of you. And, Bruce, man, you know you're my best friend in the world. But I'd really like to spend more time with you, Anamika. Alone. I think given our, uh, prior relationship, we owe that to ourselves. I need to, anyway. How does that sound?"

Anamika and Bruce nod their heads. Anamika smiles at him.

"And there's more. Bruce," Jonas twists his shoulders toward Bruce who's sitting next to him. "I don't know what's going on with Anamika and I either. Or what might go on. I don't know what the rules are here, you know, the friendship rules. The bro rules."

Bruce laughs affectionately. "'Bro rules.' Ha! Never thought I'd hear that come out of your mouth, my friend. Have you been watching *How I Met Your Mother* re-runs on Ramu's computer? And I believe it's 'the bro code.'"

Jonas laughs too, with relief. Relief that Bruce is responding so warmly, and relief that he said what he needed to say. What had to be said.

"Seriously, though," Bruce adds. "Don't worry. We're all in this together, right?" Bruce looks from Jonas to Anamika in the dark. "I think we just have to let it unfold. But, hey you two," Bruce squeezes Anamika's hand. "Be gentle."

When the rickshaw stops at Anamika's apartment, Jonas, feeling bold now, asks if he could come in for a while, if it's all right with Anamika. And Bruce. Bruce looks somewhat taken aback, but agrees, and after he kisses Anamika on the cheek, the rickshaw takes him away.

In Anamika's apartment, the digital clock on her shelf reads 11:11. Anamika says something under her breath.

"Did you say something?" Jonas asks, and wonders why it so often seems to be 11:11.

"Just saying hi to my mom."

"Is she here?"

"Yup. In a way."

Jonas waits for more.

"She died at 11:11, and ever since then, when it's 11:11, a part of her and a part of me meet. To touch base, if you like."

"Should I leave you two alone?"

Anamika chuckles. Then stands very still. It looks like she's listening.

"Would you like to meet her?"

"Uh, sure."

"Okay. Sit down. Close your eyes and just relax."

Jonas's body sinks into Anamika's chair, but he feels himself floating. His body feels weightless, as if he's part of the air, and he soon hears the strains of a melody coming somewhere from a distance, through an opening in the air. He turns his attention to the song. It's a woman's voice singing in a warm contralto, and it's getting closer. Jonas recognizes the song, Jobim's "Quiet Nights of Quiet Stars." As her voice fades away on the last line, he feels himself return to his body. He is suffused with a feeling of love and sadness mixed together, and he sighs and opens his eyes.

Anamika has her eyes closed and a faint smile on her face. She looks very young, like how she must have looked as a little girl. When she opens her eyes they are wet, and a tear spills out. Jonas gets up and puts his arms around her.

He murmurs "Thank you" into her hair.

Later, over tea that Anamika makes in a pot on her hot plate, she asks him if he met her mother.

"You didn't know?" Jonas asks.

"No, I wasn't sure. I felt openings, but I couldn't tell if you went through any. It felt like you did, though. Well?"

Jonas tells her of the song that he's always liked, and recalls some of the lines he heard the woman's voice singing, her mother's voice, he assumes.

"Oh, how lovely! My mother loved to sing that one at the piano. Our livingroom window overlooked the mountains and the sea, like in the song," Anamika exclaims happily. "You're both musical. I guess you guys somehow chose that arena in which to meet."

She gives him a light, affectionate hug. "Yup, that was her all right. I'm glad you met."

"Anamika, but was it really her? If you don't mind. I'm not sure I get it."

"I barely get it myself. And it's hard to put into words. But okay. I'll try. Will you listen with all of you, Jonas?"

Jonas nods and takes her hand and holds it on the table.

"It was a part of her, like a fragment of her whole and unique consciousness, that appeared to you. It was an expression of her Self, even though it wasn't the 'real' person who lived 'before' in time coming 'back' now. There is no time anyway. There is no real person." Anamika thinks for a moment. "You know that many-faced crystal I keep referring to as a metaphor for the whole Self?"

Jonas nods. He's listening with all of himself. His inner senses are wide open.

"Okay. In her role as my mother, she was showing me one face of a crystal— in other words, I was perceiving that particular face from where I was standing in my role as her daughter, that is, in relationship to myself. That crystal face was turned to you now, just for a moment. You briefly caught the light shining on it, and the song played through the rainbows dancing in the air."

Jonas understands what she is saying on many different levels. He feels as if he's filled with multi-colored light. And the light seeps through his body and filters throughout the room, indigo and violet. Anamika's face looks transparent and lit from within, and her features begin to shift and change fluidly, almost imperceptibly: he glimpses her as a little girl with long braids and a gap between her front teeth; then she quickly transforms into a woman with white hair and a deeply wrinkled face; then a dark-skinned girl with a wide, flat nose and generous, smiling mouth; and a man with a long face and nose and serious eyes. His face.

CHAPTER 29

namika wakes up with Jonas still sleeping beside her. She had invited him to stay over, and they just cuddled sweetly in her bed until they fell asleep. She gazes at his face. She hadn't noticed before how long and thick his eyelashes are. And his lips are full and sensual, almost feminine. She's struck by the combination of edgy masculine and sensitive feminine in his face. And how it all adds up to something very attractive that Anamika finds both sexy and comforting at once. He reminds her of an American movie actor she likes, a good one, but whose name she forgets—someone who has little moles on his face like Jonas. He still looks serious, though, even in his sleep. Something tugs in her heart, and she feels love well up. Jonas. Dear Jonas. Who are we together? Who will we be to each other in this shared lifetime? Anamika gets out of bed quietly, careful not to disturb Jonas's slumber.

As she's showering, scooping water over her body from the plastic bucket, Indian-style, she recalls the man from the restaurant waving his finger in her face and telling her to go home. Even here, she thinks. Even here my words provoke anger in people. Well, in one person that she knows of here, anyway. That's a contrast from Vancouver, where almost every time she spoke about what she knew, she was called a "cold-hearted bitch," among other much worse names that she has mostly forgotten. Why? Because she said that even those who are, say, born horribly disfigured or into abject poverty, or those who are victims of abuse and terror, or those who have had terrible tragedy visit them—all of these good people who have had bad things happen to them have *brought it all into their lives for a reason.*

There was the time she was followed home from work by a man who was a regular at the bar. She had always liked him, and often joked with him about this and that while she poured his scotch neat. Then she got a bit drunk after her shift and got careless in her conversation. She let her mask fall and revealed her real self. During the short walk home, she managed to stay several steps ahead of him and just made it to her apartment building and inside the front door, which locked behind her, while he stood outside yelling drunkenly that he would rape her good and see how she liked it.

You want it, babe, ain't that right? That's what you're saying, right? C'mon, let me in and I'll give you what you want. I'll stick it down your throat until you choke on it and you'll never talk again. Bitch!

Other voices ring in her ears, and Anamika pours water over her head, trying to drown them out.

You're telling me that it's my fault that my husband used me as a punching bag? Go fuck yourself, sister.

You're saying that my five-year-old nephew who's dying of leukemia wants that? That's the most cruel thing I've ever heard in my life. Who are you, anyway?

What kind of fucking insane crap are you spouting about 9-11? That there was some kind of mysterious subconscious agreement among the terrorists and all the people who died? Who let you out of the loony bin? They should lock you up and throw away the key, you sick fuck.

Anamika dries herself off. She feels dirty now. She examines her face in the mirror. Why did she come to India? She thought she came here because she didn't want to hide her real self anymore, was tired of playing the chameleon game, would rather be by herself. But here she found more than she could ever have imagined: people who are open to unconventional interpretations, uncommon truths. People who are open to her—who want to actually listen to what she knows, even learn from her! And she found her own gifts in this: the use of the arts—like writing, dancing, drawing, sounding—to help others find what they know inside. And she found Bruce. And Jonas. She found another part of her Self. Anamika smiles at her reflection. People supposedly go to India to "find themselves." She kind of did that literally.

She makes a few faces in the mirror. Lifts her eyebrows dramatically, one at a time—a talent both she and her mother shared. It came in handy in the theater. Wiggles her ears. Curls up her top lip. Grimaces as widely as she can. Tries grimacing, ear-wiggling, and eyebrow-lifting all at once. Then bursts into laughter.

Okay, so maybe it's all really very simple. Maybe she came here just to escape the bullies. And to learn how to say what she means, to "speak her truth" as they say, in a more welcoming environment. And to get people writing and dancing and drawing—to help them bring what they were learning about themselves into their bodies, to bring it home. Maybe it was time she brought it home, too. All of it. Including this new way of being with people, this expressive artsy way. Maybe she won't have to pretend anymore, even in Vancouver—now that she's discovered how she can be with others while also being true to herself. She can shed her chameleon skin once and for all. Dance herself right out of it.

She shimmies into a purple kameez, and as she walks out of the washroom, she flicks her long damp hair over her shoulder and gives a little skip. She says an inward thank you to all of those people in Vancouver whose miscomprehensions and rage helped bring her here. And she thanks the angry Indian man at the restaurant who gave her the instruction she needed. Because now she knows it's time to go home. She's going home.

~

Jonas wakes up when Anamika is making breakfast. He watches her buttering naan for a while. Every movement she makes seems elegant to him. He feels like he's observing a beautiful dance. A breakfast-making dance.

"What's for breakfast?"

"Jonas, you're awake!" Anamika walks over to the bed and crouches beside it.

The thin purple kameez she's wearing clings to her small, upturned breasts, and her damp hair falls in her face.

Jonas takes his hand out from under the bedsheet and gently brushes her hair back. Anamika's dark almond eyes seem to see right into him, and as they look into each other, Jonas feels an unmistakable stirring beneath the sheets, down in his body.

He pulls her onto the bed beside him, and their mouths meet. Slowly, sweetly, lips on soft lips, his tongue a question mark that gets answered by hers, they explore the place where their words come into the air, moist, rhythmic.

Anamika sits up and pulls her kameez over her head. Heat fills Jonas suddenly, painfully, as his eyes rest upon her light pink nipples that cap her gently pointed breasts like limpet shells. And he brings his mouth to them and hears her sigh like ocean waves on a night shore.

Jonas becomes immersed in the waves of her body and swims into her most sacred subterranean cave, tasting her delicate salts on his tongue, finding the pearl resting in soft folds just outside. He kisses this treasure, and his tongue coaxes it further out of its resting place until its full beauty is exposed.

His fingers take her pearl and polish it gently, slowly at first, up and down, then in a circular motion, then up and down again, listening carefully to her sounds, taking his cues from her gulps and gasps and groans, as she sinks into the ocean and rises up again for air. The pearl shines, glistening. His tongue dips in and out of her sacred cave that is filling with ocean water.

And when he is full of her savor, his mouth travels up her waving body, pausing here and there, up to her limpet-shell nipples, and he bathes them in her own salts and sucks her flavor back into his mouth as her nipples magically harden and point straight up. And her small hand finds his own hardness, and she clings to it like a life buoy, grasping it, and begins moving up and down its entire length, and he feels his tide rising, and he hears sounds all around him, a storm, and she is guiding him into her sacred cave, dripping now at its opening, and he slides inside her and she surrounds him.

They rock together, one body of ocean pounding the shore, and waves rise and fall, and the storm swells, and Jonas hears the sharp cries of birds, the howls of wind, the moaning of mermaids, and Anamika arches into him and their eyes open and meet and they crash into each other in long waves.

Afterward, they lie together, limp and slippery as seaweed washed up on the shore.

About twenty minutes pass in luxurious, spent silence, while Jonas and Anamika make the slow return to the separateness of their bodies. The scent of the sea surrounds them.

"So. What's for breakfast?" Jonas asks again, grinning.

He leaves after a two-and-a-half-hour breakfast, during which Anamika told him that she was ready to go home to Vancouver and could arrange to get on the same flight as he and Bruce, and Jonas told Anamika of his need to know which spiritual path he should take. She felt a bit mystified by Jonas's apparently overwhelming concern. But then, she has never had the experiences with a guru that Jonas has had. She has never had a teacher, period. Well, not outside of what she finds in herself. She doesn't see herself as being on a "path" either—and whether it can be called "spiritual" is a matter of debate.

Although she often turns inward and sometimes finds a beautiful empty peace there, at other times her inner experience opens into other dimensions of consciousness, creativity, and connection. She hasn't a need to be one with God or to be "free"—she already feels almost *too* unfettered and finds that she needs occasional grounding. Sometimes meditation gives her that grounding. And she just isn't concerned with matters of ultimate truth. She knows all she needs to know about what's true, and lives there comfortably. If there is "more," she's content to discover it when she's ready, when it comes up for her. Maybe it's coming up now?

Although she didn't mention it to Jonas, she sometimes sees enlightenment as yet another dimension of consciousness, a wide one, free of interpretations, not physical. When the apparent limitations of physical reality are seen through, it's a whole other ball game.

In India, the magical and multidimensional aren't questioned; they are a given. There's a good reason why in North America superheroes are comic book characters and in India they are gods, she thinks. The attributes of superheroes and gods are similar: they are each ubiquitous in their respective cultures, children want to be them, and adults' imaginations get fired up by them. But in the rational West, superheroes are considered childish fantasy, whereas in India the gods are a staple of daily life; they are everywhere. Everyone knows their crazy stories by heart—learned them as children, but not from comic books— and praying to your favorite ones will give you what you need. Anamika likes that. She sees India as the pineal gland of the world.

Anamika wonders if and how she can help Jonas find what he needs to. Ah, Jonas. Making love with Jonas was right up there with the most mind-blowing experiences of her life. It was a bit of a surprise, too, that they even found themselves in that kind of embrace. Anamika doesn't believe in soul mates: it's too rigid a concept for her. There are many souls and many mates and it's all beautifully malleable. But now that sex has appeared on the stage, Anamika knows with a certainty that their lives will continue to be very much entwined. And she is happy about this. Really happy. Jonas seemed pretty happy, too.

After she and Jonas acknowledged that their relationship has a definite romantic element, Jonas walked home to talk with Bruce about what was going on. He wanted to do that on his own.

Anamika hopes that it will go smoothly with Bruce. She puts away the breakfast things, gets on her scooter, and drives, not knowing where she is going. She drives past temples and down dusty streets and finds herself at the place where she used to sleep on the side of the road in the early days of her time in Tiru, nearly six months ago now. The place where she became Anamika.

Around her are the usual scruffy orange-robed, matted-haired, long-bearded sadhus, squatting by the side of the road, some of them smoking beedies. A couple of them recognize her and nod cheerfully, flashing near-toothless grins. She bums a beedie off one man she recognizes and squats and smokes with him. She became adept at the Indian squat when she hung out here—it took some practice before it became a comfortable pose—but now she's rusty. Her calves and thighs begin to ache.

"Anamika." She hears a soft, deep voice behind her, and turns. A few feet away is the sadhu who gave her that name! Her name. He approaches her quietly as Anamika gratefully stands up, and they look into each other's eyes for several seconds. A smile begins to form under his moustache and spreads across his entire face, disentangling the wiry hairs of moustache from beard. "Anamika."

"Baba," she responds, putting her palms together in a heartfelt Namaste, and bowing her head respectfully. When she looks up he is already walking away, fingering his string of mala beads in one hand, the sandals on his feet making scratchy sounds in the loose gravel on the side of the road.

She gets back on her scooter and drives home, the throaty *Aaauuummmm* of her scooter's motor parting the air. She got what she wanted. She went back to the beginning, where she started out, and she found her goodbye. Thank you, India.

CHAPTER 30

Jonas needs to be quiet for a while before seeing Bruce. He comes across a small roadside temple on the way home, leaves his flip-flops on the street outside the entrance, and walks in. It's dark inside and cool, and Jonas can make out only one figure, a man in a white lunghi sitting beside the gold-painted statue of Ganesh who is garlanded in orange marigolds and surrounded by little candles and burning incense. Jonas sits down on the smooth tile in front of Ganesh, folding and tucking his legs beneath him—in hero's pose, as they say in hatha yoga. He doesn't feel like much of a hero right now, knowing that he'll soon have to break his best friend's big heart.

He's always liked Ganesh, the friendly-seeming elephant-headed god who removes obstacles and is the patron of the arts and letters. And the god of new beginnings. As Jonas sits and looks at Ganesh, he feels a familiar heaviness in his base chakra at the end of his tailbone, and then a dull ache. He welcomes this feeling and dives into it, letting the sensation clear his mind, letting it connect him to the vastness outside and within himself, letting himself fall away. He sits until the pins and needles in his legs and feet become painful and interrupt his meditation, and he rises, bowing to Ganesh before he steps out into the bright hot light of the Indian afternoon, slips his feet into his flip-flops, stomps the remaining tingles out of his feet, and walks home.

"Jonas, my man!" Bruce is sitting at the little kitchen table, on which rests a tall bottle of Kingfisher beer and a stainless steel bowl full of cigarette butts. "Welcome back!" Bruce's voice is loud and overly jovial. He is obviously drunk.

Jonas pulls up a chair opposite him, still feeling a calm in the center of his body. He doesn't speak.

"So, where were you last night, buddy? Like I need to ask?" Bruce lights a cigarette, exhales forcefully, and takes a long swig from the bottle. "Oh, where are my manners. Would you like a beer?" He nods to a few more bottles upright on the floor.

"Sure, thanks." Jonas says quietly, and opens one for himself. They drink in silence for a few minutes.

Bruce squints at Jonas through a swirl of cigarette smoke. "What was his name again?"

"Whose name?"

"The asshole who stole your wife."

Jonas closes his eyes. Of course. He has the sensation of something folding in on itself, returning to its source.

"Sebastian."

"Yup, Sebastian. Or The Fucker, right? Isn't that what you called him? The Fucker?"

What I called him before I experienced his pain, Jonas thinks. Before Jonas's perceptions, his past, changed. Before everything changed. Before India.

"Bruce, I'm sorry."

Bruce guffaws.

"I didn't want to hurt you. You know I love you, man. You're my best friend. I...I...we...couldn't help it." Jonas hears Sebastian in his words. He realizes that he's saying the exact same things Seb said to him years ago. Damn. Was there any other way?

And Jonas's calm center splits apart like a dam breaking, and a red river floods through his body, his very cells, and it hurts, and all he can hear is the rushing of the river, his blood in his ears. He watches Bruce stand up suddenly, knocking his chair backwards and flinging his empty bottle across the room. And now Bruce has his face right in his, and he can't hear what he's saying but he watches his mouth form shapes that look like anger. And Jonas stands up and then he's on the floor on his back and the rushing in his ears, in his heart and brain, is too loud and then it stops.

When Jonas comes to, his head hurts and he hears a very high, thin sound inside of it. He sits up slowly and wipes his nose with the back of his hand. Blood. He feels wetness on his chin. More blood. He tries to stand, but his head is pounding and might explode. He lies back down. The floor is sticky. He is alone.

"Thank you all for coming. I want to begin by telling you that I'll be giving only a couple more satsangs because I'll be returning to Canada in a week. The schedule for the remaining meetings is on the notice board." Anamika recalls Ramu's sadness when she told him earlier today that she would be leaving soon and not working for him anymore. She feels emotion well up.

There is much murmuring and a few intakes of breath.

Sita's voice is almost a whisper, but Anamika hears it clearly. "Oh, Anamikaji, I am very much missing you and these satsangs. It is such a blessing in my life. What will I be doing now after you are going?"

Anamika swallows, and her eyes fill with tears. "Oh, Sita, you are a blessing in my life also. I am certain you will be just fine after I am gone. Continue to sing and dance!"

Sita smiles a little sadly at that, and Priya puts her arm around her mother.

"Let's begin this evening with some sitting in silence." Anamika drops deep into her body and settles there. She lets her emotions go. And somewhere she sees a few sparks that grow brighter and larger until they are filling up her consciousness with white electricity, then they disappear into darkness. She feels the room grow heavy in meditation and sinks into it for a while.

"When you're ready, open your eyes and we'll begin. Yes. Hello," Anamika nods at a couple of latecomers. "Welcome."

"Lately I've been having conversations with my friend about the differences between what I speak of and what Ramana Maharshi and his guru-disciples teach." Anamika stops talking, noticing for the first time that Jonas is not here. Neither is Bruce. This is the first satsang that Bruce has missed since she began giving them. She senses those sparks again, at the edges of her consciousness, and continues.

"There is a truth that cannot be escaped, no matter which path you walk down. And that is how everything you see, everything in your life, your world, your body, is a reflection of yourself. It's all about you. Period. You create it all. You see it when you believe it. And you don't do it just for the hell of it, or even the fun of it. You do it to learn, to grow, to work out your shit, to become more of your whole Self. You do it to see that you do it. And to see how and why. And like anything in life, the greatest gifts for you are in the most hard-to-reach places."

So Jonas isn't here, Anamika muses, just when the satsang topic comes from his questions. Just when the answers seem to be finding language in her voice, for the first time. She finds this interesting and important. *Where are you?*

"And once you truly see that it's all you, the play looks different. Now this is where the non-dualist tradition and I might part company. In the non-dualist way, when you see through it all—and wake up from the dream-play—you see that it was never you doing anything, but that it was all happening anyway, that it was, and is, all God. There is no need to do anything because you never did in the first place. And you rest there, at home in the nectar of your Self that permeates every little thing." Anamika pauses and closes her eyes.

"Oh my, that sounds nice, doesn't it? Truly." Anamika sighs. "Mmmm... I think I might have converted myself here!"

A few people laugh at this.

"So here's the difference. In my world, I do stuff—not only my personality 'I,' or the ego, but my greater 'I'—and there is rest, sure, but it's intermittent. And maybe it is for an awake being, too. What do I know about it, anyway? Or maybe there are degrees of wakefulness. Stages. I've heard of some enlightened gurus who still have challenges in physical reality, who seem to get caught up in it from 'time to time.' And then there is Ramana, who, as I understand it, lives outside of time and space, and whose presence, whether embodied or not, seems to open in those near him another state of consciousness, a glimpse of infinity. Miraculous stuff. Powerful. Real. As I'm sure many of you sitting here know."

There are nods of agreement, and a few heads bend toward each other to engage in brief, whispered conversation.

"I can transcend the physical, as enlightened beings do, but for me there are levels and layers of experience. And this is joyful to me, and wondrous. An awake being finds joy resting with All That Is, in the bliss of being with God—or, to be more precise, discovering that she was God all along. Well, I too find joy in being God! A creative kind of joy. I can see the paintbrush in my hand and relish the vibrant colors that splash on this canvas and that one.

"Here's the thing, though. If you speak that seemingly 'new age' adage—that you create your own reality—many people can take it in a facile, overly simplistic manner: that you, as you are, can and should be able to attract whatever you want into your life. And most people want stuff like love, fame, power, and wealth. Supposedly, you just need to learn a few techniques. Make an attitude adjustment. Easy-peasy. And if you don't get what you want, you're doing it wrong." Anamika pauses and takes a breath. "But it doesn't work that way.

"First you need a larger perspective, you need to sense the fullness of who you are, and live there—and then you see that it's not your personality per se that attracts things into your life, but you as an aspect of your whole Self. There are many levels to this. And it's not about attraction, but rather creation—artistic creation. You are an artist, always engaged in your work. You just need to learn to take a step back and take a look at your painting. It's a symbolic representation.

If there's something you don't like there, understand why you've included it. Interpret the symbols. Then you can alter it.

"So, the question might be 'To do or not to do?' Do you follow Ramana and sit still and quiet and become detached from the stories and the doing? Or do you get involved in doing things in the world, creating and joining community, living life 'to the fullest'? Here's what I say: it doesn't matter. Either works. Or both. Mix it up. Do or not do as much as you feel comfortable with. If it's all God doing everything anyway, so be it. If you, your Self, have a hand in it all, that's cool too. But…but you must take a step back regularly and see the whole picture. And see the hand that's making it. If you don't do this, you'll be forced to do it at some point anyway—through what might appear as sudden tragedy, illness, heartbreak, depression, death. What poet said 'The world is too much with us'?"

Kris pipes up, "Yeats? Keats? No. Wordsworth, I think. Yes."

"Thanks, Kris. Yes. When 'the world is too much with us,' we will be brought back to ourselves. Your Self. You will have to go inside and see how it really is. You will be forced to stop. And look around.

"When I first learned about Ramana, I was interested in his use of the word 'Self.' And in one of my first satsangs, I was asked if what I speak of as the whole Self is the same as Ramana's Self. At the time, I said that I didn't think so. My whole Self isn't God or All That Is. But now I wonder about a few things.

"Perhaps Ramana's Self is indeed what I call the 'whole Self,' and perhaps 'waking up' is making a shift to the timeless, multidimensional perspective of the whole Self, the totality of all of one's incarnations, the crystal turning in the air. Becoming one's whole Self transcends all imaginable, and even unimaginable, limitations. I also wonder if All That Is, or God, is perhaps really the totality of all of our whole Selves—the universe of constellations, the ocean of sparkling crystals. All of us in all of our glorious multifaceted-ness together.

"Maybe God is even more. Maybe the whole is greater than the sum of its parts. Or does the whole not exist without its parts? After all, without the dancers, there is no dance. Is God the dance? Or is each part a whole in itself, containing everything within it? Each face of the crystal a crystal itself, reflecting the entirety of the whole, and each whole crystal refracting and reflecting the light of the surrounding crystals, and on and on. Fractals and mirrors.

"Whoa. Okay. Whew. I'm getting dizzy!"

Anamika takes a deep breath. She feels that she's trapped herself in a tortuous maze of words. She wants out, but can't find the way. She's brushing up against the ineffable, the fundamental paradox. Perhaps she has gone too far in this dual-path business. Doing, not doing. Does it really matter anyway? Does it matter just to Jonas who isn't even here? She feels like Jonas now, trying to touch truth with words and thoughts. Her head hurts.

She hears a high, thin sound, and sees those sparks again, and they are dancing, and then something cracks open. Light seeps in, and in that light there is a message that is as clear as day. She's not sure if she sees the words or hears them or if they are being imprinted inside her body; and she knows that this is how Jonas feels when words come to him from somewhere else. So she just speaks what is coming to her.

When you paint and sing and dance and write, you are where you are at this very moment. It's all the same. There is also the wisdom of the breath and stillness, and the paradox of immense creativity that pours forth in all whose channels are open wide. It's all about the opening here, becoming the hollow bone, the bamboo—for through the open one, the listening one, all is given freely. So it is both *a surrender and a creating.*

As you know, this is everything: the physical shapes you see, the people around you, your body—it's all living art, an expression of who you really are, and its purpose is to allow you to see the painter's brush in your hand. The closer you get to acknowledging who is making the art, the closer you can be to joy—the freedom that knows no boundaries of time and space and death, for it's all an ongoing gentle birthing of vulnerable beauty, tender and generous, as the love between mother and child.

*All love is creative and regenerating, and the love of Self is the same. That's what
we all need reminding of. Sitting still is part of that. So is making art in phenomena.
Both together they are the means to open the channels and let the breath move freely
throughout the body, the blood flow in the veins, the rivers move in your dreams.*

~

Jonas is floating in a river, letting its current carry him who-knows-where. He
is buoyed up with immense trust; everything is as it should be. Nothing really
matters. The river lightly caresses his body that is barely there. He is not Jonas,
but part of the moving river. And look! He is moving the currents himself now;
and now he is froth on the water's surface; and now he is a fish with wide-open
eyes staring through wavering ribbons of green underwater light to a school of
tiny minnows; and now he is a minnow swimming so fast all he feels is a rush
around him. And now he understands fully and for the first time: it is *both* a
surrender and a creating. Why didn't he know that before? Its truth is in the very
river. As clear as day.

And now he is sinking into the river, his body gathering around him like
a weight. He is letting go of it all. His body, his life. He lets himself sink down,
down into the quiet dark. Everything is as it should be. And a woman's voice parts
the water molecules: *Where are you?*

Jonas starts, gasping for air. His eyes flash open to the grey ceiling of the
apartment. His head is one dull, throbbing ache, and his body is stiff. Where is
he?

He sits up slowly. Stale-beer-and-cigarettes smell. Patches of dried blood
on the floor. He remembers. Overcoming nausea, Jonas gets up and, steadying
himself on anything he can find, makes his way to the toilet. First he pukes, then
pees, then looks at himself in the mirror. Holy shit, he looks bad. Black blood
around his nostrils and smeared all over his chin stubble, swollen purple on the
bridge of his nose and under one bloodshot eye. He washes his face gently, and

touches his nose. Not broken. Some of the dried blood is caked on good and he uses Bruce's washcloth to rub it off.

Bruce. Where was he. How long had Jonas been out. He looks out the window. It's dark outside.

Jonas finds a Coke in the icebox and sits on his mattress with his back against the wall, long legs stretched out, enjoying the pressure of the hard glass bottle on his lips and the sweet bubbly cool prickling the back of his throat. He wants a cigarette, but they are way over there on the table beside the overflowing bowl of butts. He isn't thinking about anything. Not yet.

The room is especially calm after Anamika finishes speaking. She gazes around the room, and as she does, something changes. There are no separate people in front of her, around her, but one bright ocean, shining, limitless. It is all at once overwhelming, huge, powerful and oh-so-intimate, personal, soft. Intensely alive. Indescribably beautiful. Loving. She has never been here before, but it seems as if she's always lived here. Am I home? Am I this?

She feels these thoughts elsewhere, unimportant, and not coming from anyone. They could keep rolling on and it wouldn't affect anything, wouldn't cause a ripple in the ocean. They are like snippets of an overheard conversation in the next room. Disembodied. Not requiring attention. There is no attention anyway because there is nothing to attend to. There is nothing but this shining eternal ocean.

Anamika speaks, and she hears her words, but they don't come from her. They seem to be pulled effortlessly from the beautiful ocean.

There is nothing to do except to feel who you are. There are no philosophies; there is just this. You are this.

~

At the foot of Jonas's bed, something is shimmering, amorphous patterns of light are shifting, rippling, reflected from something moving like water, now taking shape, gathering into a form. And D's image appears, and Jonas hears his soft-spoken words but not through his ears.

There is nothing to do except to feel who you are. There are no philosophies; there is just this. You are this.

And D's image morphs into Anamika's, and she is speaking the same words, her image superimposed on D's so Jonas sees them both at once. And D and Anamika are speaking in harmony, the notes of D and A, the beginning and end notes of a chord, the D chord, on his guitar, sweet music. He is somewhere in the middle between D and A, part of the chord, of D, harmonious, whole, playing, filling the room.

And the ocean that Jonas swam in once before opens to him again, and he knows he never really left.

~

The ocean is sparkling with bright white crystals on its waves, and each crystal becomes distinct and elongates into its own obelisk shape, and at the top of each one Anamika sees several faces all at once, superimposed on each other. Then they spin into each other, a turning crystal, until all the faces of each crystal blur into one face per crystal, and the ocean disappears. And each crystal becomes a person sitting in the room around her, casting colored light through the others, radiant.

"How very beautiful you are." Anamika feels words arising in a body, and now it's her body again, separate from the other crystalline bodies in the room. And as she sees them as separate from her, so they become that. And now they are only glowing with a soft light, these people who are also her, reflecting her own light back to her. Many of them are smiling. She is smiling.

Anamika gets up from her chair and goes to the table on which she keeps paper, pens, and pencils, and she hands them out. Maryam gets up and helps her distribute them as Anamika talks. She knows she is repeating what she's said before several times, but repetition is good for understanding. And besides, now there is a different angle to add.

"Who is seeing through your eyes? You can never see yourself. We never see ourselves, either physically or how we seem to others. Why is that? And because of this, we are fascinated with how we appear to others. We study ourselves in the mirror, in photos, in videos our friends post on Facebook and Instagram. Is this how we appear to others? We are concerned about how others interpret us, our behavior, if they think we are good at what we do, if they see us as talented, kind, or intelligent. Why are we so concerned about this? *Because we want to know who we are. We are always seeking ourselves.*

"Who is looking out? Who am I?"

Anamika is aware that her previous "Just Me" teaching is now colored with Ramana's "Who Am I?" self-inquiry. It's all coming together for Jonas, Anamika thinks.

Once everything is distributed, Anamika returns to her chair.

"Write for five minutes about what you see in this room. Pay attention to everything, not just the visuals. What is here?"

After five minutes pass, Anamika gives another instruction.

"What else is there? Or what else is here? Five more minutes to write about this."

Five minutes later, Anamika speaks.

"Now draw what's in this room. Draw it over your words, or turn the paper over, or get another piece of paper. Ten minutes."

"Finally, I'd like you to give your word-art vision a title. Five minutes more to complete it to your satisfaction and give it a title."

When it looks like everyone has finished, Anamika says, "Now, if you like, share your work with someone sitting close to you. Let's do this for twenty minutes, then take a break, and we'll regroup in half an hour."

Anamika walks out of the room, making her way through people alight with words and images, through waves of paper being exchanged, ripples of laughter, swells of conversation. She walks outside into the night air, and breathes deeply. The air tastes salty. A familiar figure approaches her through the dark, tall and skinny with a messy mop of long hair, turning in from the street, stepping a little unsteadily in his flip-flops. Anamika embraces Jonas silently. When they come apart, she sees his bruised face in the moonlight and touches it gently, her fingers butterfly wings.

CHAPTER 31

When Anamika goes back inside the room with Jonas, they see Sita standing at the front of the group, talking animatedly and laughing. She seems to be leading a discussion. Her face is flushed. Jonas and Anamika linger at the back of the room and listen to the comments flying about in the air.

"How can it be that it is so different?"

"Maybe it's not the same room!"

"Of course it's not. It is different to each of us."

"How many rooms can there be?"

"Your drawing makes me smile!"

"Is that me there?"

"There are one, two, three, four…"

"I don't understand your meaning."

"Are your words about you or the room?"

"What's that, love?"

"There can only be this one room."

"No-no, this is not true. This is not what Anamika is teaching us."

"About me, of course. It's just me."

"Twenty-five, twenty-six, twenty-seven…"

"Where do you end and the room begin?"

"Good question."

"Who are you?"

"There is no room."

"I am new here."

"It's all the same anyway."

"Thirty-five, thirty-six! There are thirty-six rooms!"

"But this part here, this is what I saw, too."

"Me too."

"It has to be different, right?"

"Who says this must be so?"

"It's all just energy."

"Oh, you're counting people! Look, there's Anamika."

"Does anyone have the time?"

"I am what I see."

"I see what I am."

"Ha! I see what I am!"

Jonas lowers his body carefully into an empty chair at the back, and Anamika makes her way to the front.

"Oh, Anamikaji!" Sita looks like a little girl who's been caught doing something naughty. "Sorry-sorry. I am forgetting myself." She plops herself down on her cushion quickly, and it makes a little *fsssst* sound in the quietening room.

"Sita, but it looks like you're having so much fun leading the group! No need to sit down."

"No-no. Thank you, Anamikaji." Sita takes a big breath. "But, if you don't mind, I am wishing to say one more thing to my friends."

Anamika nods encouragingly to Sita who stands up again, smooths her turquoise sari, and faces the group.

"I want to be thanking all of you for all you are giving to me," Sita says solemnly. Her eyes are moist. She places her hand over her heart. "I am filling up with thank-you's for everybody here."

Maryam speaks from where she sits. "Sita, you have become my good friend, and Priya, and many of you here. I would like to express my gratitude to Anamika and to all of you for sharing this experience with me."

"Yes, for Kris and I also," Gabi joins in. "We are happy to have learned so much from such a great teacher, and to have made so many good friends."

"This is very true," Kris adds, placing a hand on his heart and bowing his head. When he straightens up, he looks around, grins, and says, "If you ever come to Frankfurt…"

Sita sweeps Anamika into her arms and holds her tightly. Anamika's face is buried in Sita's bosom, and she can smell the rose oil perfume in the silk of Sita's sea-green chula. When Sita bends down to sit on the cushion once again, she touches Anamika's feet reverently. Anamika doesn't feel embarrassed this time.

After satsang, Anamika and Jonas walk to where Jonas has been living with Bruce, and Jonas gathers his things up in his backpack while Anamika cleans sticky beer and blood off the floor, gathers up the beer bottles, and empties the ashtray bowl. It looks like Bruce hasn't been back. Jonas is starting to worry about him. He expresses this to Anamika as they walk to her place, where they have decided to stay together until they leave India. They hold hands as they walk.

As they approach her apartment, they see someone sitting on her front stoop. It's dark, but Anamika knows it's Bruce. She recognizes the silhouette of his large frame and wavy hair, and the feeling of power in his body, even from a distance. She remembers seeing him there for the first time, when he gave her a box of barfi. The sun was shining, and he was a sun god. Has it only been a few weeks? It feels like lifetimes.

She glances at Jonas, who swallows, his prominent Adam's apple moving up and down his neck, and she squeezes his hand. He sees Bruce too.

Bruce stands up as they draw near, and Anamika unlocks the door and the three of them enter.

"Shall I make tea?" Anamika asks over her shoulder as she heads to the little kitchen area.

Bruce and Jonas stand awkwardly just inside the door. Jonas shrugs off his pack.

"Come in, if you like. Sit down." They continue to stand.

"Anamika. Jonas." Bruce's voice is hoarse and quiet, and he's looking at the floor. "I am so ashamed."

He turns to Jonas and raises his eyes. "I'm sorry."

Jonas looks at Bruce and sees himself. "I'm sorry too."

"You have nothing to be sorry for." He studies Jonas's face. "God. Did I do that to you? I barely remember."

"Yeah," Jonas smiles a little.

"I haven't hit anyone since I was a teenager. I was drunk. Well, you know that. Drunk and angry. Fucked up. No kidding, right?"

"Right."

"Does it hurt bad?"

"Not anymore. Just feels tender."

"Fuck. Forgive me. Please."

"Sure. I already have."

"Anamikaji?" Bruce turns to Anamika, who is putting cups out on the table. "Do you forgive me?"

Anamika walks over to Bruce and puts her arms around him in response. The muscles in his back feel tight, hard. He barely hugs her back. He is keeping himself contained.

The three of them sit down at Anamika's table, like they did at Bruce's table after Jonas reconnected with him and met Anamika, and they all had such a great time together drinking Kingfisher beer and talking about Vancouver. So much has changed. And Vancouver is just a week away.

Bruce lights a beedie, and clears his throat. "I've been trying to figure out what to say. Here goes. Anamika, I love you. You know that. I think it's the first time I've really been in love. And I get it. I get that you and Jonas are together; I get that I can't do anything about that. It hurts like hell, but maybe I'll get over it. Maybe I won't. Maybe it's what I need right now. To go through this. I dunno.

"But I can't hang around and watch you guys be happy together. I'm just not that enlightened, I guess. I've cancelled my return flight, so I won't be flying home with you. I'm heading north to Rishikesh the day after tomorrow, traveling with Maryam. We're going to catch Mooji's satsangs. Word is that he's there now."

CHAPTER 32

Jonas and Anamika sleep together, intertwined. They sleep long and deeply. Anamika dreams that she is in Vancouver, in a sunlit room with deep blue walls, sitting on a chair in front of a small group of men and women, some sitting on the floor on cushions and some on chairs, who are all writing and drawing quietly together. There are several pieces of large blank paper taped to the walls, a plastic tarp on the hardwood floor beneath each piece of paper, and jars of brightly colored paint and paintbrushes on a long table nearby, beside a basket full of small percussion instruments and peacock feathers. The room is vibrant with creative energy.

Jonas dreams that he is in Vancouver also, in a quiet room with light green walls lined with bookshelves. He is sitting at a table in front of his computer, and outside the window to his right is a view of the mountains. He is writing a book. He is also in India on retreat with D, sitting in the open-air meditation hall in the ashram, at the foot of the holy mountain. The words fall out easily from his fingertips onto the screen, the tapping on the keyboard making sounds like water falling, and he is carried along by them as if they have always been there, waiting for him. He can hear Anamika moving about in the kitchen, making tea.

Jonas and Anamika wake up together in the hot light of a late Indian morning. It's 11:11. As Jonas looks at the glowing red numbers on Anamika's digital clock, he sees the lines of the four "1"s elongate, stretch up and down, and each of the "11"s becomes a long path that doesn't end, and there are two paths, joined by two dots of light. And two words from his dream, from his book, come to him: *The Mountain*. And he knows what they need to do.

The next day they wake to the alarm set to 4:30 AM. They put their water bottles and a few snacks into a daypack, and after breakfast they get on Anamika's scooter. Jonas directs her to the ashram where he went on retreat with D, and she parks the scooter just inside the gate. They watch the new pink glimmer of light in the sky from behind Arunachala. The ashram grounds are empty of people, but in the dawning light, Jonas sees a few peacocks roaming about. One of them meows. Jonas laughs and puts an arm around Anamika. It's cool in the dawn air. The perfect time to climb the mountain, before the heat of midday.

He takes her past the lotus pond to the open-air meditation hall, and they sit together quietly on the cold marble floor. Jonas closes his eyes and feels the space fill with the sangha and with the presence of D. Behind his eyes, an image of D appears sitting on the dais, and he can hear the warm, soft sound of his voice. *Welcome.* Jonas feels a tear slide down his cheek. As they leave the fragrant air of the meditation hall, Jonas puts his palms together in Namaste, in the direction of the dais. Anamika does the same. And Jonas is filled with such love for her that he thinks his heart might fly out of his chest.

He leads her past the little cottage that was his home for two weeks, and past D's cottage, pausing for a little while at each place. Remembering. Feeling that Anamika was always there with him, as she is now. Here. They leave the ashram grounds and take the path Jonas used to walk to the mountain at dawn, after morning chai in the dining hall. They walk past the stone well where Jonas felt himself fall until he felt no fear. They walk past the house with the rooftop patio from which he saw his name miraculously etched on the side of the mountain. They walk through the farmer's field and find their way to the base of Mt. Arunachala. And they begin their climb as the sun peeks out from behind the mountain.

They climb silently through the dry scrub, on dirt and rock, sometimes coming upon a path made by the footsteps of those who had walked this way before. They walk upon whatever path they find. There are many paths. Many ways to climb the mountain. In one rocky area, they find a natural cave, with a fresh stick of incense burning outside. Halfway up, they stop under a small tree and eat crackers and drink water. The air is getting warmer now in the early morning light, and is filled with birdsong.

Jonas and Anamika reach the top of the mountain at mid-morning. It's already hot. They splash water from their bottles onto each other's heads and laugh, happy to have made their way to the top of the mountain. Happy to have made their way to each other. They find a large boulder jutting out, and they clamber over it to its edge and sit down cross-legged. They breathe. They breathe in "here" and breathe out "now." They can see the entire lay of the land, everything, stretching out every which way they look. What a view.

ANAMIKA'S EXERCISES AND MEDITATIONS

If you'd like to experience Anamika's exercises and meditations for yourself, here they are.

1. Opening Scene Exercise

Close your eyes. Imagine that a friend of yours wants to watch a movie, and selects one that has your name in the title. You've clicked Play. The movie opens. What is the first scene? Write it or draw it on the paper. Don't think about it. Just do it. In five minutes.

If you wrote about the scene, now draw it, and vice versa. Five minutes.

Finally, give your movie a title. Remember: it has your name in it. Two minutes for this.

2. Novel Interpretation Exercise

You read books. I know, because you've read this one. When you read, say, a novel, you know it's not the "real world." If it's good, you might get lost in it, suspend your belief for the sake of the experience. It becomes real to you, in a way. And reading the novel becomes another experience that is yours and that you can share with others who have read the same book.

Just for a minute, imagine that your life, your world, is like a book you're reading. A good book. So good that you may have already forgotten that you're creating it all. You've suspended your belief for the sake of the experience. You may indeed believe that it's the real world.

You are the main character, the protagonist, of course. Look around you. Those objects, that person, even that tree, are there for a reason—to create an atmosphere, support the plot, lay the framework for action, draw a scene. Look at your hands that hold this book; they are shaped a certain way, beautifully drawn, unique to you. You have expressed the shape of your hands, your body, the features of your face, just as you have expressed everything you see, every situation you're in. It's an intimate and ongoing art project, and that hand you see is in everything.

Just for the heck of it, put this book down for a minute. Only close your eyes this time.

Welcome back. Here's a little writing activity for you. Give yourself five minutes for each part, and don't stop writing. Don't worry; no one will judge you. No one will even read it but you. This is for you. Just you.

How would you describe the scene you're in now? Don't forget to pay attention to mood and atmosphere.

If your book-life had three major themes, what would they be?

What are the three main struggles of the protagonist?

3. Other Lives Exercise

Hold your pen loosely in your hand. Keep a sheet of paper beneath it or nearby. Now close your eyes and sit any way that feels comfortable. Let your thoughts leave your mind. Don't push them out—just let them go. There is nothing at all that needs your attention right now. Nothing. There's nothing to do, nothing to remember, nothing to think about. If a thought enters, tell it you'll deal with it later. Clear a space. A large, empty, peaceful space. Just sit for a while in it.

Someone is now coming into the space. Can you feel the presence, maybe see him or her? Feel comfortable. There's nothing to fear. In a real way, it's just you.

Put your pen on the paper. Don't think. If a word or image comes, write it down. Just follow it wherever it takes you, one word or image at a time. Don't anticipate. Don't do anything yourself. Don't try.

4. Song-and-Dance Meditation

If you are in a group situation, feel free to trade movements with each other.

Do you have room to stand up and move around a little? Good. Imagine you are standing waist-deep in a warm ocean. Move your arms slightly away from your body, and back and forth, letting your fingers run through the water around you. Feel the electric tingles at the ends of your fingers.

Now let your arms move any way they want to.

Now let your whole body move any way it wants. Let your feet move, your hips, your torso, shoulders, head. Feel the dance move through you.

Is there a sound in your body? Let it come out. You are composed of sound, and your vibrating cells sing to each other. Your fluid body is singing like a river. Let the song of your body come out.

5. Medicine Exercise

The supposed physical "cause" of your illness doesn't matter. What does matter is what it means to you. What part or system of your body is experiencing the problem? How do you see this body part or system? In your own personal mythology, what does it symbolize? Interpret the metaphor of your illness. Once you do that, and if the interpretation feels right to you, there will be a shift, a transformation. Only when our wounds are revealed can they be healed.

If you are unwell, here is an exercise that will help promote wellness. Get yourself into a comfortable position. Now turn your focus on wherever you feel discomfort—your chest, your sinuses, your leg, your hip, your guts, your head.

Go inside of it. Experience the feelings there as fully as you can. Sink into the feelings. Deeply. As deeply as you can. And just stay there for a bit.

Let whatever images that are there come forth. Watch the image, let it evolve. What does it look like? What color is it? What is its shape? Does it have a texture? If words come out of the feeling in your uncomfortable area, say the words; if there are sounds, make the sounds. If you want to make a movement, a gesture, do so. Let your body speak to you in whatever way it wants. Listen and watch carefully for its messages, then express them in whatever way feels right. Do this for a few minutes, then stop.

Now breathe fully; feel the breath throughout your entire body. Concentrate on your full breath for a few minutes. Then go back into the discomfort and find what's there again. See if it has changed. Alter the expression you made before to reflect this new state. Do this for a while, then stop. There is a world inside your body. Be an explorer! Take the risks you need in order to find what you're looking for.

If you are sick, and you spend a bit of time each day on this, listening to your body and what it has to tell you—heeding its messages—there *will* be changes, and you will feel better. You will begin to recover.

Your body is your own, an intimate reflection of yourself. Your body is the best teacher there is. The resolution to the problem is in the problem itself. The medicine is in the illness.

6. Listening Meditation

Listen to the sounds in this room, the sounds from outside, in the sky, in your body. Just listen for a while.

It's really all about listening. Everything is. Being compassionate is being a listener. Compassion is love listening. Being aware is being a listener. Awareness is Self listening.

Listen with your inner senses. Open your listening self until all you are is listening. When someone speaks to you, like I'm doing right now, try listening this way. Don't wait to speak; don't track your reaction; don't provide an internal commentary; don't anticipate what the speaker might say. Don't think of yourself at all. Don't even think. Just listen. Listen with all of you.

7. Just Me Meditation

This meditation is especially useful in those times when you feel overwhelmed by the world and people, when you are overcome with worry or regret, or when you wake up in the middle of the night, your mind buzzing with uncomfortable thoughts.

Close your eyes. Imagine that it's just you sitting in a room. Just you, alone. There's no one else here. It's just you in a room by yourself. You don't have to think of anyone else. All relationships fall away. Take a deep breath and let it out slowly. You have no thoughts of anybody. Why should you? It's just you. Feel the relief that comes with knowing that. Ahhhh. Breathe deeply through your nose from your belly, up through your lungs, and out through your mouth. What a relief. It's just me.

There's just me here. Say it to yourself. Like you mean it. Just me. That you know it's just you, there's no one else around, no one to watch you, to make demands on you, to judge you—no one to deal with in any way at all. There's just you alone in this room.

Just me. It's just me. There's no need to think about it. No need to think about anything. I know who I am. I am comfortable with myself. So comfortable. I love myself. It's just me here. No one else. No one else anywhere. What peace. It's just me.

Feel the relief of knowing it's just me. Whew. It's flooding my body. I am calm and quiet. It's just me. Just me.

8. Just Me Exercise

This works best if the Just Me Meditation is done right before.

When you feel ready, open your eyes. Pick up the pen in front of you. Write for five minutes about how it feels to know it's Just Me. Don't stop writing, let your pen move across the paper. Write in any language you are comfortable in. This is just for you. It's just you here. It's all about you.

Now I'd like you to bring a relationship you have with someone into your consciousness. There is the person you have this relationship with. Envision the person. Notice how that feels in your body. Where in your body is this feeling? Keep breathing.

Now let's write once more. This time, write for five minutes non-stop about how you see this person. Write from that place in your body. If you don't know how to start, imagine that you are walking down a street and you see the person walking toward you. How does she or he look? What do you feel in your body and what do you think about as you see him coming toward you? Tell a story about him, if you like.

Now you have two pieces of writing about yourself. Even that story about the other person is really about you. Sometime tomorrow or the next day, take a look at these two stories and compare them. Read them as being about the same person. And see what you have told yourself in them. If you want to write about what you have discovered, go ahead.

9. Stillness Meditation

Just be quiet and still for about ten minutes or so. Close your eyes if you like, and go inside for a while. Don't look for anything; just notice. And notice how when you notice something, it disappears. Watch whatever is there—your thoughts, feelings, aches and pains—pass by like clouds in the sky. Like leaves on a river.

10. Self-Compassion Meditation

Turn that compassion you feel for others onto yourself. You've been through a lot. You're going through a lot.

If your eyes are closed, keep them closed. If not, close them if you like. Feel the beautiful calm in the room right now. Now feel what's inside of you right now. Is there a place where something uncomfortable or painful is living? Has something recently come up? If so, find it now. Look at it if you can, see the images or sounds attached to it. Don't relive the experience. Just observe it as it exists inside of you right now. Keep breathing. Let's stay with the observation for a few minutes.

Now, if you're ready, feel into it. Feel past whatever anger for someone else may be there—past whatever may have been done to you—and into the hurt. Just feel it. Feel it *gently*.

And now let it know that it's welcome here. This pain is a child, a hurt child, you as a child. Let your compassion enfold it. This is nothing but a beautiful thing. You aren't prodding at a wound, you are looking at it and acknowledging it. Bathe it in warm, healing water. Bathe it in your compassion.

Now put your palms together at the center of your chest, as if you were saying Namaste, as if you were praying. If you like, bow your head a bit. And just sit like this for a while.

Feel the respect you have for yourself. Everything you do, everything that you've done, has been good enough.

Finally, feel the unconditional love you have for yourself, and especially for that little child inside of you. So sweet, so vulnerable. She did nothing wrong. She just got hurt.

11. Seeing Exercise

Who is looking out of your eyes? Who am I? To answer, write for five minutes about what you see around you. Pay attention to everything, not just the visuals. What is here?

Now write for another five minutes: What else is there? What else is here?

Now draw what's around you. Draw it over your words, or turn the paper over, or get another piece of paper. Ten minutes.

Finally, give your word-art vision a title. Five minutes more to complete it to your satisfaction and give it a title.

If you like, share your artwork with someone else here. Notice the differences. Notice what your art tells you about who you are.

12. Here-and-Now Meditation

Close your eyes and get comfortable. Feel the breath move in your body. Concentrate on it. Breathe in "here." Breathe out "now." Keep doing this until it becomes unnecessary.

SUBJECT GUIDE TO ANAMIKA'S TALKS

ACKNOWLEDGMENTS

My heartfelt gratitude to the thoughtful readers who provided feedback—Penny Short, Diane Stiles, Lynette Harper, Brad Zembic, Soressa Gardner—and to the other readers who gifted me their enthusiasm; to Atma Frans who helped get me started; to Sacred Stories for getting the book out there; to Devaji for the inspiration; and to Adam Potvin for being my son.

ABOUT THE AUTHOR

Janis Harper is a writer, singer-songwriter, actor, and former adjunct English professor turned expressive arts therapist. Her writing can be found in literary journals and anthologies, including two creative nonfiction anthologies that she conceived and edited: *Body Breakdowns: Tales of Illness and Recovery* and *Emails From India: Women Write Home.* She has presented her work in Canada, the US, and India, and lives in British Columbia.

A mystic with a philosophical bent, at 14 years Janis was chanting for an hour a day in front of her Buddhist shrine; at 17 she was reading the Seth material and experimenting with channeling; at college she took all the religious studies courses available. As an adventurous young adult, she traveled a lot and lived in other countries. Later, as an academic in Rhetoric and Composition, she explored how language creates reality and taught writing for many years at college and university in Vancouver, BC. She has also enjoyed a long though intermittent career as a performing singer-songwriter and stage actor. (Her CD *Better This*

Way is available online). In midlife Janis shed academia and became an expressive arts therapist, helping others to access their own creative resources for healing, transformation, and self-discovery. She has always been in love with India, but didn't make it there until later in life. On one of her many long visits, she found an enlightened teacher at the foot of Arunachala.

Janis's lifelong passions for the creative arts, metaphysics, spirituality, and philosophy come together in *Jonas and the Mountain*. Although fictional, she considers it to be the truest work she's ever written.

janisharper.ca

CPSIA information can be obtained
at www.ICGtesting.com
Printed in the USA
BVHW041757080622
639178BV00003B/6